She wanted to hurt him as he had hurt her...

"Changed your mind, Clarissa?" he asked softly.

She didn't answer, but instead moved her lips along his shoulder, willing herself to keep cool as his arms tightened around her.

There was a laughing glint in his eyes as his lips met hers, and for a moment, the force of his kiss so overpowered her that she felt she might drown in him. She pulled away abruptly.

"See you sometime, Mr. Publisher," she spat. "Thanks for all the good things you've done for my brilliant career. And my sexual awakening!"

"What do you think you're up to?" Rage contorted his face.

"Oh, a little lesson in love — " she looked unmoved " — I thought it was time you saw it from the other side."

New Discovery

Jessica Ayre

Harlequin Books

TORONTO • NEW YORK • LONDON
AMSTERDAM • PARIS • SYDNEY • HAMBURG
STOCKHOLM • ATHENS • TOKYO • MILAN

Original hardcover edition published in 1984
by Mills & Boon Limited

ISBN 0-373-02641-2

Harlequin Romance first edition September 1984

CHAPTER ONE

CLARISSA HARLOWE opened the office door soundlessly and stopped short. The broad-shouldered figure behind the smooth mahogany desk had his back to her and was barking down the telephone. One hand played havoc with a crop of bristling white hair.

'I don't care how many copies it sells,' the voice rapped. 'I won't bid that much for a piece of utter rubbish!'

So this was the tone editorial directors of enormous publishing conglomerates took in the privacy of their offices! Clarissa was seized with a sudden desire to laugh, but she muffled the instinct and instead closed the door silently behind her, gazing for a moment at the plaque which boldly announced, Garrett Hamilton, Editorial Director.

She didn't know quite which way to turn now, but decided on the direction away from the one she had come, away from the ansaphone which had instructed her to proceed to Mr Hamilton's office. These fully automated New York offices distinctly left something to be desired. Glad of the thick carpet which muffled her footsteps, Clarissa found her way towards what she concluded was a waiting room. Rows of books lined the walls and a long coffee table displayed what she supposed were new publications. With a thrill she noticed her book among the others. The objective existence of her own persistent scrawlings, so solidly bound between covers, always filled her with astonishment. Out there was a piece of herself she no longer quite recognised, made even stranger this time by its American garb. She moved to finger the book, open it at random to see if the words made any sense, and she wondered what the American reviewers would make of it when it was officially published in several weeks' time.

A hoarse voice behind her startled her from her

musings and she turned to find a small dark-haired boy staring at her intently.

'I'm Ted,' he offered. 'Who are you?'

Clarissa identified herself and the boy continued to gaze at her with unblinking eyes. She attempted some small talk, but suddenly he stopped her, his eyes growing wide with wonder.

'Are you a punk?' he queried.

Clarissa burst out laughing and pulled a hand through her thick auburn hair. 'Not as far as I know,' she smiled at the lad, who continued to stare at her with evident curiosity.

'But you are English?' he said at last.

'Very much so,' she nodded. 'But the two things aren't necessarily the same.'

A mischievous smile appeared on his face from nowhere. 'I think I'll do a picture of you,' he announced.

'All right.' Clarissa settled into the comfortable leather armchair and watched the short, still pudgy fingers clasp a pencil, the intense concentration on the smooth face as the little boy carried out his task.

'There,' he said after a moment, 'I've done you as a cat, 'cause you have slanted eyes with yellow speckles in them and your hair's all bristly and furry.'

Clarissa looked at the drawing seriously.

'You mustn't be insulted,' the child added. 'I do everyone as animals. I'm a chipmunk in pictures.'

'May I keep it?' Clarissa asked. 'I like it very much.'

The boy nodded and tore the sheet from his pad, just as a tall brunette, sophistication written on every fingernail, entered the room.

'Oh, there you are, Miss Harlow. Mr Hamilton is waiting for you,' she said, giving Clarissa the distinct impression that Mr Hamilton should never be kept waiting for anyone.

Clarissa moved to follow her, tucking her bulky manuscript under her arm and waving goodbye to the little boy. He threw her a wistful look. 'I wish you could stay with me and play.'

'Now, Ted, you leave Miss Harlowe to her work,'

the brunette chided.

Shrugging, Clarissa gave Ted a comic, conspiratorial look and waved again, thanking him for his drawing.

She followed the swish of the woman's hips down the corridor and thought how lucky she was to have bumped into the child. It had stopped her from nervously pondering why she should suddenly have been summoned to the almighty Garret Hamilton's office. Although she had had numerous meetings over the months with her immediate editor, Elizabeth Ascher, she had never before received a summons from above. And from what she had heard over the grapevine, Hamilton was not someone she would get on with. He was meant to be one of those New York publishing marvels, a sacred monster who made and destroyed lives as rapidly as he ate and spewed out books. The phrase 'a blend of literary tact and hard sense' came to her mind. She must have read it about him somewhere, Clarissa scoffed. Given what she had overheard of his telephone conversation, hard *cents* would be more like it, and plenty of dollars!

Nonetheless, she tried to smooth her habitual light trousers and tee-shirt into some order before confronting him. And she heartily wished that she had had some advance notice of this meeting, rather than simply being ordered upstairs when she presented herself at Elizabeth's office.

The secretary announced her and withdrew. But Clarissa's progress into the room was cut short by the sight of the man heading towards her, hand outstretched in greeting. Despite the shock of unruly white hair, Garrett Hamilton could not have been more than thirty-four. His head was one of the most striking Clarissa had ever seen. With its dark brows over slightly hooded, fiercely blue-black eyes, straight nose, flared nostrils, and determined jaw, it had at once an elegance and a wildness which reminded her of a Renaissance portrait. Her tongue froze in her mouth, and even when he had released her hand from his firm grasp, she couldn't quite manage a greeting.

A smile curled round his full lips without quite reaching the watchful, intelligent eyes. 'Miss Harlowe, I know it's a chore for young writers to meet an editorial director, but I can assure you, I'm not the monster some make me out to be. Do sit down and stop gaping at me. Let me get you a drink.'

The blatant arrogance in the man's tone set Clarissa's adrenalin racing, and as she watched him stride confidently across the room, pour drinks and then return to lean on the edge of his desk, his long legs stretched indolently in front of him, she had the overbearing sense that this man could only mean trouble. She took a long gulp of her drink and perched expectantly at the edge of her chair, ready to defend herself against him.

Garrett Hamilton surveyed her lazily, his arms crossed over his muscular chest. 'You're even younger than your photographs, Miss Harlowe. We have a child star on our hands!'

Clarissa pounced, some of her tension relieved by the verbal effort. 'I'm not interested in being a star, Mr Hamilton,' she said coldly. 'I'm a writer.'

Hamilton chuckled while his eyes mocked her openly. 'So it would seem, Miss Harlowe. A first novel already a critical success in England and soon to come out here. A prize-winning book of short stories. And now . . .' he looked meaningfully at the bulky package she had placed on a corner of the desk, 'I gather there's a second novel. Quite an achievement for a young woman!'

Clarissa's eyes flashed daggers at him, but she could find nothing sensible to say in reply to his accurate inventory.

The smile played round his lips as he noted her edgy silence. It seemed to amuse him, spur him on. He stretched further back on the desk, half leaning on one arm, and examined her reflectively from beneath thick lashes. 'You know, I've always wanted to meet a flesh and blood version of Richardson's heroine, a live Clarissa Harlowe.'

Clarissa could feel the smattering of freckles round her nose stand out against the whiteness of her skin—a sensation she always had when she was about to erupt.

'Is that why you've summoned me here, Mr Hamilton? To examine a specimen? Well, it's a waste of both our time. I can assure you I have none of the original Clarissa's tremulous nobility. And I have no intention of being victimised by heartless rakes of any description,' she added emphatically.

She realised from the mischievous tilt of his eyebrow that her comment had only tickled his humour further.

'So it would seem from your work, Miss Harlowe. Not a rake to be found anywhere!'

'It's not a subject which interests me,' Clarissa replied, her voice laced with contempt.

With a shrug of his shoulders, he moved suddenly to the chair behind his desk. The face before her now bore quite a different expression, like a mask which had been pulled out from nowhere at a moment's notice.

'Since neither of us have much time to waste, Miss Harlowe, let me tell you why I've summoned you here—as you so aptly put it.' His eyes seemed glazed with boredom, and his voice took on a professional staccato. 'I like to meet new writers who interest me, who are likely to become part of the Jethrop stable.'

'Like some highly-strung thoroughbreds,' Clarissa muttered, hating his tone.

He caught her words. 'Just like that, yes,' he said coldly. 'Rearing authors is no less risky than rearing horses. And the rearing in this case,' he added in clipped tones, 'involves a lot more than gentle editorial persuasion. There's a whole marketing and promotional apparatus to bring into play. And that's the second reason I've summoned you. I've decided that we're going to back you to the hilt—especially if this new novel is good. Interviews, radio, television, a foreign rights push, the lot. We'll make you into a name on everyone's lips.'

Clarissa knew that professionally she should have been thrilled by his words, grateful at the attention the firm was paying her. It was more than a little unusual for a young writer of 'serious', indeed 'experimental' work—as the English critics had tagged it—to become the subject of large-scale, or any scale, promotion. But Garrett Hamilton's air of bestowing favours from a great height simply made her feel like some randomly chosen object of institutional charity. Now his cold gaze anatomised her, part by part. She knew he was visibly assessing her media value. 'And what do you think, Mr Hamilton? Do I have the necessary star qualities?' she snapped at him.

'You'll do,' he replied coolly, without ceasing his inspection of her. 'You'll photograph well. Electric, fashionably cut hair; wide catlike eyes which could be made up to extraordinary advantage'—he met them for a moment and Clarissa shivered—'a seductively mobile mouth. Figure's not too bad, a little boyish perhaps, but we'll have you get some clothes to show that off to better advantage. Though the hermaphroditic look is probably right for the current mode. And the English accent, that's the best of the lot. It'll wow them.'

Clarissa leapt to her feet, her temper at boiling point. The man was impossible! 'You can keep your promotional favours, Mr Hamilton, and bestow them on another horse! I prefer to remain anonymous, keep myself to myself and retain just a little dignity. Goodbye!' Breathless, she turned on her heel and marched from his office.

'Thanks for leaving your manuscript behind for me to read, Miss Harlowe,' his voice rang insolently behind her. 'I'll be in touch in a few days. I'm sure you'll think differently on the publicity issue after you've had a chance to sleep on it.'

Clarissa slammed the office door and cursed the man. He had made her behave like an unreasonable child, and given that all power lay in his hands, it was the more unethical of him, she thought confusedly. Oh, how she yearned for her fatherly British publisher! Whatever had induced her to give her new book to her American publishers first, she simply didn't know. And her manuscript! she gasped. *He* would be reading it before it had a chance to be revised. She felt as if by sheer carelessness she had just allowed a new born lamb to be thrust on to the sacrificial altar. And this self-styled god, in his total lack of feeling, his crass insensitivity, would crush it ruthlessly to make it palatable for the market place.

In a confused panic, Clarissa almost retraced her steps to his office in order to steal the manuscript from his desk. But no, she couldn't face him again. Elizabeth—Elizabeth would have to sort it out. After all, it was Elizabeth Ascher, with her warm humour and endearingly scatty ways, who had urged her, since she was living in New York for the time being, to work directly with Jethrop House. So it was Elizabeth who would have to get her manuscript away from that man with his cold, superior ways.

Clarissa prodded the lift button angrily, reminding herself that it was time she called this swift, silent box, which arrived at the umpteenth floor with no hint of movement, by its proper name. Even a provincial Englishwoman should be able to tell an elevator from a lift and a monster from a man. Pushing past the sleek receptionist who guarded the tangle of offices among which Elizabeth's was one, Clarissa attempted to make some sense of how she would report her meeting with Hamilton and explain to Elizabeth that it was imperative for her to redeem her manuscript. Not only that, she didn't want, she simply *couldn't* confront the media.

But Elizabeth's greeting told her she was already too late.

'Garrett just rang to say your manuscript is being copied and will be with us in a few minutes.' Elizabeth kissed her warmly on both cheeks and gave her a reassuring hug. 'I'm so pleased Jethrop House has decided to put its full marketing power behind you.'

Clarissa took in her pretty face—which always seemed far too girlish for its wrinkles—and blurted out, 'But I don't want his eyes on it! He's odious, overbearing and odious. I won't be subjected to him! And as for the rest . . .'

Elizabeth patted her shoulder. 'Don't worry, hon. He's a wonderful editor and he'll grow on you with time. I don't know the woman who's been able to resist him yet. Just wait until he turns the charm on.'

'Charm! If that's what you call charm,' Clarissa snorted.

Elizabeth looked at her reflectively and shrugged. 'You've obviously started off on the wrong footing. Funny, I thought you'd like each other. He's superbly intelligent, you know. The best we've got.'

'You're the best you've got,' Clarissa interjected, almost in tears.

Elizabeth smiled, her face creasing into feathery delight. 'Never mind, honey. It'll sort itself out, and despite what arguments there may have been between you, gearing up the promotional machinery can only mean good news for your work.'

Clarissa glared at her. 'You too?'

'Yes, me too. Just be a good girl and assume we know what's best. It can only hurt for a few weeks.'

'So you agree to my making a stupid spectacle of myself? What on earth does it have to do with writing?'

Elizabeth looked at her calmly. 'Nothing at all, Clarissa. Nothing at all. But you write in order to be read—and in the dear old U.S. of A., all this scurrilous publicity business assures that you do get read.' She smiled a reassuring smile. 'So settle down and we'll make a trip to the publicity department to meet the man who's handling you. We've left all this a little late in any case, since the directive from above only came this week. There's no time to lose.'

Clarissa groaned, 'All right, you win. But if it backfires and I can't put a single word on paper for months, it'll be your doing.'

Elizabeth patted her shoulder again. 'Persistent scribblers like you don't dry up after a few confrontations with the camera, Clarissa. So be a good girl and come with me.'

Clarissa trailed after her recalcitrantly up a flight of stairs towards Greg Lahr's office, tucked tidily away into a corner space between four other publicity people. Greg was one of the two to handle fiction, Elizabeth explained, and their director preferred to team women writers with Greg.

Despite this spurious piece of publishing strategy, Clarissa was relieved, indeed pleasantly surprised when she set eyes on Greg. He was a lanky young man with blue eyes deeply set in a handsome, slightly equine face and with a manner so ungrudgingly enthusiastic that Clarissa took to him immediately.

'I think you're great,' he said instantly, and although she realised he must say this to all his writers, she nonetheless welcomed his crooked smile and warm handshake. 'I've read your book twice,' he told her, 'as well as the English edition of the stories, and I know exactly whom to send the novel to for review. In fact, I've done most of that already. But now I need to find out a little more about you, to get a handle on you for the interviewers and TV people. Shall we have dinner tonight?'

Clarissa nodded and smiled at the barrage of words. It seemed she was going to get caught up in the publicity mill whether she liked it or not, so she had better learn how to cope.

After Greg and Clarissa had confirmed details of meeting places, Elizabeth ushered her back to her own office. 'Now, young lady, a few words from me. No hysteria in front of the interviewers—just a lot of calm Englishness and repeated mention of the book's title. But Greg will fill you in on all the standard techniques. More importantly, I'm throwing a party this weekend at the Connecticut house. All the media bigwigs will be there. It's not a promotional party as such. Nothing that crass—but it *is* meant for you. We've put the word round subtly for the time being about this brilliant young English writer. So they're all waiting to meet you.'

Clarissa gasped. 'I can't, Elizabeth! I hate parties. I'm hopeless with new people.'

'Well, you'll have to learn quickly. You don't need to say much, just look beautiful and mysterious and sound very English. That shouldn't pose any problems, should it?'

Clarissa groaned loudly.

Elizabeth's eyes twinkled. 'Well, pretend it's a masquerade. Listen, hon, I've got an idea.' She reached into her desk and brought out a chequebook. 'Go and get yourself some clothes—dressing-up clothes, clothes for Clarissa the actress who has nothing to do with the writer. That'll help. And don't protest—I'll put it on the publicity budget.'

Clarissa's eyes suddenly sparkled. Play-acting, yes—that appealed to her. As long as she didn't have to be herself among all these people. She met Elizabeth's eyes. Yes, she was a clever woman. She had made this whole publicity whirl possible by turning it into an adventure—like a sub-plot to be lived by one of Clarissa's own minor characters.

As Clarissa made ready to leave the office, Elizabeth's secretary walked in bearing a copy of the manuscript. Clarissa's eyes clouded over, but Elizabeth refused to let the subject come up again.

'Go and get yourself some clothes, hon, and leave this package in my care. Relax. Greg will pick you up on Friday. Bring an overnight bag and I'll entertain you for the weekend. A little country air will do you good.'

Clarissa thanked her and Elizabeth added, 'And sweetie, don't panic, we'll soon have you back at your typewriter.'

Clarissa gave her manuscript a last lingering look. By the time she was in the lift again, her momentary calm—due almost wholly, she realised, to Elizabeth's reassuring presence—had vanished. How had she allowed herself to be railroaded into this horror of a publicity exercise when she knew very well that she was only happy dreaming in front of her typewriter.

It was all that terrible man's doing, that Garrett Hamilton with his arrogant, overbearing ways. She was sure he cared nothing at all for writers or their work: he was simply in the business of making commodities take off, launching new monthly packages of cornflakes—except that the packets contained books, people's entire lives. She shivered as she walked through the luxurious anonymity of the Jethrop House lobby. This very place made her irritable, with its high arched ceilings and creamy marble walls. All the hushed solemnity of a cathedral, she thought morosely to herself, calculated to make the individual feel wholly insignificant in the face of some awesome power. Her mouth curved into a wry smile. But here, the awesome power was the gigantic publishing structure—its innumerable parts from editorial to production to promotion and marketing—dwarfing the single solitary writer who, nonetheless, was the cornerstone of the edifice.

Clarissa thrust her shoulders back in an effort to overcome a mounting sense of her own irrelevance and stepped through the holy portals on to Third Avenue. A wave of sultry heat enveloped her. She had all but forgotten the clinging warmth of the day in the artificial atmosphere of Jethrop House. Now it engulfed her in dizziness and she decided not to walk back to SoHo through the streets she had so grown to love. Instead she considered for a moment and turned in the opposite direction. Bloomingdales was only a few streets away. It would be cool inside, and she might as well get the inevitable over with and buy some clothes as Elizabeth had instructed. Prepare for the masquerade.

As she walked through the store's glittering displays, its innumerable small departments and hundreds of subtly arranged mirrors, she suddenly caught her own reflection and remembered Hamilton's ruthless inspection of her. She could feel the blood rising in her cheeks, and paused to examine herself through his eyes with equal ruthlessness.

She saw a slight girlish figure—boyish, he had said, she remembered and fumed—dressed to hide, more than to display. Vast, thickly lashed blue eyes slanted across her face so as almost to drown the straight nose with its smattering of freckles, the wide mouth pursed now as it investigated what appeared as an unknown sight. Clarissa chuckled. It was Ted, the little boy, who had got her right, she thought warmly. With her red-brown mass of hair, tawny skin and clothes which blended into the same shades, and omnipresent eyes, she looked like some small furry animal who had emerged from an unpeopled night into an alien environment.

Well, she was going to change all that now. With a dawning sense of excitement, she ruffled through racks of evening dresses and turning on her writer's eyes, she determined to clothe her character appropriately. A few minutes' search brought the perfect garment to hand: a simple fawn-coloured silk which rustled gently, its strapped camisole top delicately embroidered with a single flower, its skirt flowing down to ankle length on one side and rising above the knees on the other—like some elegant thirties dancing dress.

Clarissa peeped at the cheque Elizabeth had given her and noted with a sense of guilt that it covered far more than the cost of the dress. Well, I'm going to have to work for it, she consoled herself; and choosing a creamy silk jacket that matched the dress's embroidery, she took herself off to the changing room.

The dress graced the lines of her body, delicately accentuating the fullness of her bosom and slender hips. Clarissa's eyes sparkled. Cinderella makes her debut, she smiled to herself, and went off to buy a pair of matching slippers, all the while concocting a pert, slightly raffish persona, thoroughly English in her eccentricities, who would dazzle the dull American interviewers.

In search of shoes, Clarissa stumbled on some more garments which would suit her new persona to a T, and struggling only momentarily to make peace with what she thought might be the beginnings of a hateful vanity, she indulged herself. A black silk trouser suit, cut like a man's—to suit the hermaphoroditic trend of the times, she quoted the sacred monster irreverently—fitted her to perfection, its demure strapped top calculated to give the lie to the masculine lines of the jacket and trousers. And then, with an eye to autumn, she burrowed into her own pocket and splurged extravagantly on a light brown garment of softest suede, a mini-skirt topped with a fitted jacket, its sleeves amply puffed in Renaissance style. She thought of little Ted and his query about whether she was a punk. In this get-up she needed only a little brash lipstick and she would emerge as *Vogue*'s answer to angry London!

. Pleased with her purchases and now putting the finishing touches to her emergent heroine, Clarissa walked out into the muggy late afternoon air. Long lines of traffic filled the street and impatient hoots mingled with the high-pitched blare of sirens. Clarissa glanced at her watch. Rush hour. The underground would be sweltering and there was little point in attempting to rouse a taxi. Despite her packages, she would have to walk.

She stepped off the kerb. A loud hoot resounded in her ear, followed by, 'Can I give you a lift, Miss Harlowe?'

Startled, Clarissa turned and through the windscreen of a low-slung black Porsche made out Garrett Hamilton's striking features. Before she could shake her head, he had opened the passenger door for her, and given the persistent blare from the waiting cars behind, it would be sheer madness to protest. She slid in beside him, just as the lights turned red again.

A humorous glint lit his eyes. 'I see you've taken my advice and done some shopping.'

Clarissa was ready to hit back and deny that it had been on his advice. But she controlled the flare of anger his tone seemed immediately to kindle in her.

'Oh, I'm quite prepared to be a compliant marionette if the right strings are pulled,' she offered.

He threw her a quizzical glance. 'I take it Elizabeth pulls the right strings and I don't?'

Remembering the pertness she had written into her new persona, Clarissa curved her lips into a droll smile. 'A little gentle persuasion always seems to work far more wonders than brute authority.'

He laughed, a low rumbling sound from deep in his throat. 'And I, of course, am a brute. Well, Miss Harlowe, might I persuade you, gently implore you, to place those bulky packages into the back seat.'

With a great show of compliance in response to his mannered politeness, Clarissa deposited her bundles and leaned back into the car's upholstery.

'And now, Miss Harlowe, might I beg you kindly to tell me where you would like me to deposit you and all those packages?'

Clarissa played into his tone. 'Oh, I shouldn't like to take you out of your way, kind and gentle sir. Almost anywhere that takes me closer to SoHo will do.'

'Well, then, I shall take you to your very doorstep. It's not much out of my way, dear lady.'

She indulged him with an exaggeratedly grateful look. She noticed that his returning smile had none of its previous mockery, and as he focussed on the traffic, she allowed herself to study him a little more closely. The profile was a strong one and his shoulders in the loosely fitting summer jacket he was now wearing seemed even broader. There was an easy grace about his movements as he shifted gears.

He must have felt her eyes on him, for suddenly he turned to her with a wry twist to his lips. 'And have you concluded that I have the necessary star qualities, Miss Harlowe?'

'Oh, with the right clothes and make-up, I dare say you'll do, Mr Hamilton,' she said maliciously. 'Though I think your maleness may be just a little too marked for the current fashion.' She was astounded that the words had passed her lips.

His eyes kindled dangerously, but before he could speak Clarissa had intervened with babble that covered her nervousness and told him all about how she loved New York, particularly SoHo and the Village; how Manhattan reminded her of a medieval town, all turrets and towers, surrounded by an enormous moat; how kind the pople were.

He interrupted her. 'Have you lived here long?'

'Eight months.'

'And you live alone?'

'Oh yes,' Clarissa continued to babble. 'It's the only way for a writer to live. You know, sometimes you want to stay up all night and write, if there's anyone else around, you feel you have to comply with their habits and ... I could tell you a story about a writer friend of mine who ...' She was off and running, engaged in one of those rambling narratives which in a roundabout way eventually answered the question she had been posed.

They had stopped at another red light and he was gazing at her so intently that she stopped speaking in mid-sentence. 'I'm sorry, I'm boring you,' she flushed hotly.

He shook his head. 'Most certainly not. I was just thinking that the interviewers will love you. My instincts were right.'

Something in Clarissa snapped. The man was congratulating himself! He had taken in none of what she had said, merely been watching her, evaluating his investment. 'Well, hurrah for your instincts, Mr Publisher,' she said scathingly. 'It would be nice if they extended beyond the bounds of the media drones. You can drop me right here.'

'I said I would take you home, Clarissa.' There was a threatening note in his tone.

The sound of her name on his lips gave her an odd sensation, almost as if he had touched her. The atmosphere in the car seemed suddenly to grow charged, thick, so that Clarissa felt she couldn't move.

'What's the address?' he asked coldly.

She told him and within seconds they were there.

She reached for her bags and noticed that her manuscript was lying on the back seat of the car. Covertly she picked it up, aware again that she couldn't bear this man's eyes on it until it had taken on the impersonality of print and time.

Garrett Hamilton stopped her, 'That's my copy I

believe,' he said coldly. 'I intended to start on it tonight.'

Clarissa shrugged. 'I'd rather you didn't. Read it at this stage, I mean.'

He paused and then looked at her lazily through sleepy eyes. 'Why? Will it make you vulnerable to me?'

Clarissa's eyes grew wide. 'Most certainly not,' she announced emphatically, and in a bound she was out of the car, her packages bundled gracelessly in her arms.

'Thanks for keeping me company through the traffic,' he offered, meeting her eyes.

Clarissa only stared at him, unable to make an equivalent thank you pass her lips. She stood on the kerb even after the car had pulled away, looking blindly after it, only aware that she was trembling despite the warmth of the evening.

Then with an emphatic 'Brute!' she turned to make her way up the three stairs which led to her door and dug deep into her bag to unearth her keys. She didn't even pause on her way to the fourth floor loft she inhabited to say her habitual hello to the people who ran the madcap gallery downstairs.

Only when she had thrown her packages on to the sofa and herself after them did she stop to ask herself why she had been seized by a sense that she had to escape from this man, an urge so great that it made her behave with uncustomary rudeness and altogether inappropriately, given that she suspected he could overrule Elizabeth at any time and was thus central to her future as a writer. Was it simply because he seemed to crystallise everything she feared and hated about the publishing world? Its rampant commercialism; the contradiction it so blatantly posed, particularly in America, between marketing hype and literary integrity?

Clarissa shrugged and slowly went to put her new clothes away. Secretly she admitted to herself that there was something else about Garrett Hamilton which frightened her. Something to do with the inordinate amount of space he seemed to occupy, so that his presence was inescapable; something too, about the way in which he seemed to look straight through her.

She shivered, suddenly feeling lost in the vast single high-ceilinged room which comprised her New York home. Over the months she had learnt how to be comfortable in this alien, gigantic space, lent to her for a quarter of the going rate by friends of friends. The loft belonged to two journalists away in Latin America for a year, who—in order to have their cats well looked after—were willing to rent out the place for a minimal rent. Clarissa's London publisher had arranged the let, when Clarissa mentioned that she wanted to use her prize money and some savings to live in this city, this capital of the twentieth century. But when she had first arrived in the loft, she had been stunned by its sheer size. It was so unlike her usual cosy quarters that for a month or so she had confined herself to one corner where a desk and sofa seemed to reduplicate the proportions of an English room. Gradually she had ventured out to the luxuries of the living room, with its huge wall paintings of contorted figures, its sequences of framed photographs and plush armchairs; and finally she had taken over the built-in gallery bedroom with its vast double bed.

Now, in an effort to assert her identity once more over this strange interior landscape, she busied herself with watering the hanging greenery which flourished everywhere. Then she fed the two plumply sleek cats and sat down at her writing desk.

Every day Clarissa filled a few pages of a continuing letter to her brother in London. These she posted regularly in bulky envelopes at least twice a week, and they comprised not only a chronicle of her life, but also served as a kind of imaginative diary, a testing ground of ideas.

In all the world it was to her elder brother Michael that Clarissa was closest. It was he, in a sense, who had really brought her up, guarded over her, and it was in him she confided. Her parents, though kind and probably far too indulgent, had always left the children to their own devices. Having had their children somewhat late in life, they seemed to carry on much in the same way that they had before they arrived on the scene, and though a series of foreign girls had been hired over the years to watch over the children, it always seemed to Michael and Clarissa that it was their parents who needed the looking after.

They were both artists, her mother a potter, her father a watercolourist, who lived somewhat hand to mouth, always just managing to make ends meet and never worrying too much about it. The Martello tower on the Sussex downs which the family inhabited formed a suitably dreamy setting for the two dreamers who had whimsically named her Clarissa after Richardson's heroine.

Three dreamers, Clarissa reminded herself now, as she sat musing over her letter to her brother, for she had liked nothing more than trailing over misty downs constructing fantasies about vagrant knights and richly clad ladies. It had, in fact, been something of a disappointment when the tower had acquired a bathroom and hot water, since the night time escapades to what she had called the 'dungeon' had had to stop.

She chuckled now, warm with memories of her brother and their childhood escapades in the medieval world they had dreamed. Then Michael had been sent away to school and she had been left to dream alone. It was at that time that her habit of writing to him had begun—indeed, she thought, the habit of writing itself. It was on the pages she filled that she lived her most intense life, her real life. Outside these, she was painfully shy. She had avoided making friends at school and kept herself much to herself. Then one Christmas she had discovered that she had an unexpected talent: she could act. Rehearsing for the school play in which all the children had been cast, she was startled by the fact that she could slide easily into any role given her and effortlessly become the part. Given the release of assuming another identity, she could be bold, garrulous, provocative, anything the part necessitated. And as the years went on and she went to university, she learned to adapt this talent to everyday use. So she had only to say to herself, today I need to be Portia, and she could become a competent, independent woman. Combined with her ability to tell endless rambling stories, this talent had served to mask her deeply rooted shyness, a private self which rarely came into view.

Clarissa glanced at her watch and with a start realised that if she didn't leave the house instantly she would be late for her meeting with Greg Lahr. The scathing portrait she was itching to draw of Garrett Hamilton would have to wait for another day. Mephisto, she suddenly thought. The Mephisto of the publishing world, a smooth-tongued devil willing her to sell her innermost being for fame and its cash value. We'll see about that, Mr Publisher, she challenged him silently. We'll just see about that!

CHAPTER TWO

CLARISSA stepped out of Greg Lahr's car and looked blissfully around her. It was a joy to feel grass under her feet, to see trees, tall arching oaks and maples beginning to don their autumnal coat of red. With a burst of energy, she raced across the lawn, only to turn towards the rambling white weatherboard house, with its friendly verandah, when a voice called out to her.

'Had I known you were such a country enthusiast, I would have had you down here sooner.' Elizabeth greeted a flushed Clarissa. 'Let me show you to your room and then perhaps Greg can take you for a walk through the woods. The others won't be here for a few hours yet.'

'Delighted,' Greg smiled broadly just as Clarissa was about to protest that she was quite happy to walk on her own. Much as she liked Greg, she had had her fill of chit-chat on the drive from Manhattan, and this, preceded by their dinner together earlier in the week and numerous phone calls, made it amply clear to her that, the matter of promoting her work aside, they had little in common.

As Elizabeth showed her round the small whitewashed room which was to be hers for the weekend, Clarissa took her courage in hand and dared to suggest as much. Elizabeth smiled knowingly. 'O.K., I'll take him off your hands and have him help me set up for the party. Off you go, my little solitary!'

Clarissa gave her a grateful look and tiptoed out of the house. Once out of doors, she scampered across the lawn towards the woods, like a creature released from a cage, and spent a delicious hour examining unknown vegetation, turning up strange fungi and meandering dreamily along half overgrown paths. It was with reluctance that she finally returned to the house.

Summoning up the persona she had prepared for herself over the days—the character who was going to dazzle or mystify these hordes of selfconscious Americans always on the look-out for the new—now seemed an impossible task. She lay down on the colourful quilted bedspread, closed her eyes and recreated the part for herself. The next thing she knew, a voice was calling her name over and over. Clarissa got up from her bed and made for the door.

'Almost everyone is here, Clarissa. I was beginning to worry about you.' Elizabeth looked at her in concern.

'Sorry,' Clarissa rubbed her eyes sheepishly. 'I must have dozed off. I'll be down in a few minutes.' In unthinking haste, she showered, pulled on some sheer tights and the silk dress specially bought for this occasion. Then, slowing her movements, she sat down at the dressing table and remembering the hours she had spent backstage readying herself for parts, carefully applied muted champagne and brown shades of shadow to her eyes and thickened her already thick lashes with mascara. A little creamy blusher and some tawny lipstick which only gave her mouth extra lustre, and she was ready. The composure of her reflected image gave her confidence a boost.

Following the sound of mingled voices and laughter, Clarissa found her way downstairs towards a large room whose vast picture windows brought the outdoors in. A large grey stone fireplace, a low fire kindling in its depths, seemed to have become the gathering place for a group of people from whose midst Elizabeth emerged to usher Clarissa forward. 'You look ravishing, my dear, just the thing,' she whispered in Clarissa's ear, and giving her arm a squeeze introduced her to an elderly man with a lopsided grin who turned out to be her husband, Bill. He instantly placed a tall ice-filled glass in Clarissa's hand. One sip of the bittersweet punch and immediately she was whisked off to meet more faces.

She recognised the names of several of Jethrop's more distinguished writers, as well as a few reviewers. But the names and faces blurred into an indecipherable mass and she sipped at her drink more and more nervously, hardly noticing when a second glass was placed in her hand. Luckily Elizabeth had been right. She hadn't as yet had to say much. Everyone she was introduced to had a ready flow of conversation and seemed to be far more interested in telling her *their* latest news than in hearing anything from her. One man singled her out, a tall wiry man with cleverness written all over his face. A twinkle in his eye, he drew her to a relatively quiet corner of the room.

'Elizabeth tells me you're Jethrop's discovery of the year.'

'A veritable gem, unearthed from English mines and washed up on the shores of the land of the free and the brave,' Clarissa quipped, liking the man's thin finely etched face and witty lips.

'And are we free and brave enough for you?' playfully he let his eyes rove over her body.

'Far too free and much too brave, given my last encounter with this lady,' Clarissa heard a deep voice utter behind her. She shivered, instantly recognising its owner.

Garrett Hamilton eased himself into their twosome. Striking in a creamy jacket which deepened the bronze of his face, he towered over them.

'That, Mr Hamilton, depends on how you define your terms,' Clarissa said in clipped tones, edging away from him.

His eyes pierced into her, belying the gracious smile on his lips. 'I'm pleased to see that you and Adam Bennett have met,' he said, avoiding her comment. 'Adam, as you've probably gathered, runs the most scintillating of our public television chat shows.'

'Indeed,' said Clarissa, not having realised any of this, but managing to throw Adam the most radiant of looks.

Adam chuckled and looked up at Garrett Hamilton. 'You've spoiled it, Garrett. She hadn't the least idea who I was, did you, Miss Harlowe?'

Clarissa laughed. 'I'm afraid I haven't watched any

television since I discovered that I couldn't tell the news presenters from the commercials. Too confusing! After night one, I didn't know whether I was being sold the latest missile or listening to an in-depth programme analysing the content of soap powder!'

Adam looked at her silently for a moment. 'If you promise to repeat that with just *that* degree of innocence, I'll have you on my programme like a flash.'

'All rendezvous to be arranged with Greg Lahr over there, Mr Bennett,' Clarissa smiled at him demurely. She could feel Garrett Hamilton's eyes burning into her.

'And here I thought you needed help,' he whispered sardonically, as he took her arm to lead her towards the dining room.

'Whatever gave you that idea, Mr Hamilton?' Clarissa tried to draw her arm away from those tensed fingers which seemed to leave an imprint on her. But her movement proved fruitless.

'It must have been that teenage disguise you were wearing the other day.' His eyes travelled over her dangerously.

'Disguise?' She looked at him intently. 'The self comes in many guises, Mr Hamilton—as I imagine you must know.'

The laugh which emerged from him had a bitter edge. 'Too well,' he murmured. 'Too well.'

They had reached the dining room and Adam Bennett was once more at their side. Clarissa found herself seated between the two men at a long highly-polished oak table.

Adam Bennett engaged her in conversation, but out of the corner of her eye, she saw a tall woman with luxuriant blonde hair take the chair next to Garrett Hamilton, throw her arms round him and plant a kiss full on his lips. She stole a look at the woman and at a glance took in plunging neckline and a brightly red predatory mouth. Of course, she thought, her heart suddenly beating strangely—it was Garrett Hamilton's wife. Why had she assumed he was unmarried? All

Americans seemed to be coupled by the time they left university, and there was no reason to expect the almighty Garrett Hamilton to be any different. But, Clarissa pondered as her lips moved in reply to Adam Bennett's questions, there had been something in Garrett Hamilton's manner which had led her to believe otherwise. For some inexplicable reason, the thought enraged her, made her feel like some innocent dupe.

With gestures she didn't know she had in her repertoire, she suddenly found herself slipping off her silken jacket and accepting Adam's help with a provactive movement of her shoulders. When Garrett Hamilton passed her a basketful of hot French bread, she met his eyes languorously and then, as if with a deliberate snub, turned her attention back to Adam. After glasses had been filled with a rich Medoc for a second course of lightly braised tournedos, Clarissa raised her glass to him. 'Perhaps we might drink a toast to your successful promotion of my brilliant career and Jethrop's burgeoning millions, Mr Hamilton?' she said with a tinkling laugh.

His eyes met hers with a sombre intensity and then seemed visibly to glaze over as his mouth curved into a glacial smile. 'Yes, why not, Miss Clarissa Harlowe?' With one smooth movement he was on his feet and without seeming to demand attention, he commanded silence.

'I would like to take this opportunity to welcome Clarissa Harlowe to our midst,' he stated in a respectful voice. 'Jethrop House is honoured to be publishing her first novel, *Children of Summer*, in a few weeks' time.'

Hands around the table clapped in unison and, flushing, Clarissa uttered a low thank-you.

Garrett Hamilton sat down. With an ironical glance, he asked, 'Was that a satisfactory toast, Clarissa?'

'Brute!' she murmured beneath her breath.

From under thick lashes, his eyes trailed over her bare shoulders, up her neck and stopped momentarily on her lips before responding to her look. 'Not half the brute I may yet become,' he muttered threateningly.

Clarissa shivered, as if his eyes had palpably touched her. She looked down at her plate.

In a low voice, he said, 'Now why don't you form those wonderful lips of yours round the word Garrett and stop treating me as if I were some monstrous syndicate godfather who had to be overthrown in order for the world to come right?'

Clarissa flashed him a hostile look and rudely turned her back on him, picking up her conversation with Adam Bennett as best she could, while she was so intensely aware of Garrett Hamilton on her other side. She drank far more than she was accustomed to, and by the time she had finished her pecan pie, stories were tripping off her tongue with amazing alacrity.

'Well, you've got *him* altogether spellbound,' Garrett Hamilton whispered disparagingly in her ear as they all rose from the table. 'Don't you think you might now turn your attention to another of those media men whose notice you told me so clearly you didn't want?'

She was about to lash out at him, but the sensation of his hand on her shoulders as he draped her jacket lightly round her stopped her. Their eyes locked together for an instant and then Clarissa turned abruptly to flee towards Adam who had asked her whether a little dancing after all the food would be to her taste.

The living room doors had been opened on to a wide patio and a stereo poured pulsing rock rhythms into the night air. With an abandon she didn't remember since the days when she and her brother had tried to outdo each other in the invention of steps, Clarissa threw herself into the dance, her silken dress rustling round her like a hundred autumn leaves. With a frenzy, her body tried to relieve itself of the tensions the evening had induced, and she matched Adam's ever wilder movements with her own, closing her eyes to let the music move through her.

A small hoarse voice woke her from the dance. 'I was right—you are a punk!' Ted, the little boy she had met at Jethrop House, stood in front of her, a gleeful smile on his lips. He was clad in bright blue pyjamas, animal slippers on his feet, and he looked up at her, his eyes almost as wide as his face.

'Hello, Ted.' Clarissa was momentarily surprised and then bending to his level, gave him a beaming smile.

'Can I dance with you?' His face bore a distinctly naughty expression.

Clarissa laughed, 'Of course, partner, any time.' She gave Adam a questioning glance and he waved her on.

The little boy plunged into the dance with a child's recklessness, his limbs gyrating effortlessly, his expression a parody of the many rock stars he had seen. When the music stopped, Clarissa swooped him up in her arms and cuddled him playfully. 'For a chipmunk, you're not too bad, partner,' she said in response to his grin.

'I see you've met Clarissa, Ted.' Garrett Hamilton was suddenly upon them. 'I thought you were soundly asleep upstairs.' His voice held only a slight reprimand.

'I couldn't sleep, Dad, so I snuck down.' The little boy snuggled closer to Clarissa's arms.

'And now I'm going to sneak you straight back up,' Hamilton stretched his arms out and reluctantly Ted sank into them.

Clarissa watched them both mutely, as if stunned. *Garrett Hamilton was Ted's father*! She was about to hide the tears which for some obscure reason seemed to be biting at her eyes, when the little boy called her name authoritatively and then whispered something into his father's ear. Garrett Hamilton looked at her strangely, running a hand through the thickness of his hair.

'Ted would like you to come upstairs with us. He wants to show you his chipmunk,' he said evenly.

'All right,' Clarissa nodded, and like a sleepwalker followed the pair up the stairs towards a room not far from her own.

Ted displayed his furry chipmunk to her and listed all his wondrous characteristics. Feeling Garrett Hamilton's eyes intently on them, Clarissa tried to cut short the little boy's catalogue.

'Can Clarissa come home with us so I can show her my other animals, Dad?' the little boy demanded suddenly. 'Instead of that horrid ostrich.'

'Hush!' Garrett Hamilton's tone was stern, but his blue-black eyes laughed. 'Clarissa would be welcome to visit tomorrow. If she'd like to, that is,' he looked at her expectantly.

'Oh, please, Clarissa! I'll show you the cat who looks just like you, and we can swim! Ted's excitement was tangible.

Clarissa nodded, still dazed by the contradictions she was trying to make sense of. The little boy clapped his hands and snuggled under the blankets as his father kissed him a warm goodnight. She watched the tall, lean man tousling the child's hair. It was the first time she had seen Garrett Hamilton's face relax, his eyes betray no conflict with the tensed lines of his mouth.

Something in her seemed to stir.

But as soon as Ted's light had been switched off and they had reached the landing, Garrett Hamilton's lips were once again set in their mocking tilt. 'I see you've managed to win my son over in record time.'

She was unprepared for the note of harshness in his voice, and she answered him honestly, 'He's a lovely lad.'

He gripped her arm with unnecessary ferocity. 'He doesn't usually take to people so quickly. You must have used unwonted charms.'

Clarissa looked at him oddly. 'We've met before—in your office.'

'So it wasn't just the hypnotic quality of your hips in motion,' he gave a short, bitter laugh.

She pulled her arm away from his sharply, 'Don't be ridiculous,' she murmured.

He turned her towards him and searched her face, his eyes intent on hers. She stood transfixed by his gaze, which bore a mixture of pain and suspicion. His fingers dug into the soft skin of her arms. Then abruptly, he let her go and his voice, slightly husky, asked, 'Will you dance with the father as you've danced with the son?'

Clarissa let herself be led into the cool air of the patio, her pulses throbbing beyond the small voice in her which repeated a niggling warning, 'Married—he's married.'

The music had changed now to a slow, pulsing beat, and despite her better sense, Clarissa found herself enveloped in Garrett Hamilton's arms, her cheek buried in his hard shoulder, her legs tensed against his. The tautness of him was like a shield against her thoughts and his hand on the base of her spine played against the smoothness of her dress with hypnotic emphasis. She felt herself melting into him, aware only of the fresh fernlike scent which seemed to emanate from him or the surrounding woods, she wasn't sure which, and of his chin nuzzling the thick growth of her hair.

'Shouldn't we be going now, Garrett?' a strident voice cracked the atmosphere around them. 'It's getting late.'

Clarissa looked up to see the tall blonde standing at their side. Garrett Hamilton released her gently and glanced at his watch. 'Yes, I guess it is,' he said coolly. 'I'll be with you in a few moments.'

The woman placed a long red-nailed hand on his shoulder. 'You haven't introduced me to your partner yet, not personally,' she eyed Clarissa coldly.

'Haven't I?' Garrett asked absentmindedly. 'I assumed you'd met. Bianca, Clarissa.'

Clarissa stretched her hand out to the woman, who barely let her cool fingers touch Clarissa's.

'I do think we should go now, darling. Elizabeth will never forgive us if we deprive her of all her sleep.'

Clarissa could sense his shoulder tensing, but his voice was even. 'Yes, you're right.' He took Clarissa's hand and held it for a moment. 'I'll be round to pick you up in the morning. Ted isn't very patient, once he's set his mind on something.'

Bianca shot Clarissa an icy look and Clarissa looked from her to Hamilton in confusion. 'If you're sure it's all right with . . .'

'Of course it's all right,' he cut her off. 'See you in the

morning,' and with a sudden twinkle in his dark eyes, he was off and Clarissa was left standing on the patio, not quite knowing what had happened to her.

Before she could untangle her thoughts, Elizabeth was upon her.

'That Garrett has been monopolising you,' her eyes danced merrily. 'He's fascinating, isn't he, with those dramatic features and that white hair. He tells me it's a family trait, but life has been quite shocking enough to give it to him of its own accord! Still, he shouldn't have monopolised you. I've been wanting to introduce you to some people properly all evening. Come with me, young lady.'

Clarissa trailed after her and tried to act pertly intelligent for a few more faces; but the effort was more than she could bear, and after Elizabeth had seen her yawn for the third time, she ushered her off to bed, after arranging a special goodbye for Adam Bennett and making sure she thanked Greg Lahr properly for all his good services.

'Not so bad, was it?' she hugged Clarissa goodnight at the bottom of the stairs.

Clarissa shook her head. 'No, almost palatable.'

She desperately wanted to ask Elizabeth about Garrett Hamilton and his wife, but she felt like a fool, and she wasn't altogether sure what it was she wanted to ask: How could she feel so . . . so moved—Clarissa stumbled for words even in her thoughts—in a married man's arms? Elizabeth would think her a naïve child, a blatant innocent, if she so much as voiced such a question.

As she tumbled exhausted into bed, Clarissa temporised with herself. All this emotional fuss about an illusion created by too much wine! Tomorrow, she vowed to herself, she would keep herself to Ted—a far more suitable companion for her than his acid mother and temperamental father with what was—as Elizabeth suggested—his shocking life.

The morning brought another glorious Indian summer day, but Clarissa's mood had little in common with the weather. She had slept badly, her mind racing through disjointed dreams which seemed inevitably to end in catastrophe. She refused to let herself dwell on the reasons for this, but she had half a mind to ask Elizabeth whether she could get a train back to New York and simply ring Garrett Hamilton to say she couldn't make it.

Angry at her own grumpiness, she pulled on her usual trousers and tee-shirt and passed a cursory brush through her hair, before half stumbling down the stairs. Elizabeth was nowhere in sight, but the kitchen table displayed a thermos of coffee, cereal and fruit. Clarissa gratefully poured herself a cup and brought it out on the large screened verandah. She plonked herself into a chair and stared up at the blue sky, randomly reflecting that it was far higher than an English sky, somehow much farther away. Desultory thoughts passed through her mind, all of which coalesced into a feeling of homesickness.

Damn, she cursed herself. Damn this ridiculous bout of the blues! She was about to drain her cup of coffee and go off towards the woods when a familiar black Porsche, its top now down, appeared and a child's shrill voice shouted, 'There she is—Clarissa!' he hailed her, and in a bound was out of the car and at her side.

'I told you he wasn't very patient.' Garrett Hamilton, his long legs encased in much-washed jeans, came up behind Ted and smiled a greeting.

Clarissa swallowed hard and nervously tried to put some order into her appearance. He watched her lazily and arched a humorous eyebrow.

'I think I prefer you like this,' his lips teased her. 'Less dangerous.'

'Me too,' Ted agreed, overhearing his aside. 'But Clarissa looked very pretty last night too,' he added, with the tone of an authority who was bent on defending her. He took her hand and, smiling, Clarissa squeezed his, keeping her eyes well away from his father.

Elizabeth appeared from somewhere in the house.

'Taking my young lady away, are you, Ted?' Her light blue eyes danced between their creases.

Ted nodded.

'I'll just get my bag.' Clarissa went off to her room, happy to be alone for a moment and have the opportunity to collect her wits. She remembered the scathing caricature she had drawn of Garrett Hamilton for her letter to her brother just a few days ago, and keeping this well in mind, she resolved to herself that she wouldn't again be prey to the charm Elizabeth had warned her no woman could resist. She schooled herself to her new role: Ted's friend. That wouldn't be too difficult. He was a delightful child, if a little precocious in what she imagined must be the New York way.

But as she sat next to Garrett in the car, while Ted ambled the miles away by counting telephone poles, Clarissa knew it wouldn't be all that easy. He was, she decided, being at his most seductive; a relaxed smile playing round his lips, his thick white mane tousled in the wind, his eyes a deep sparkling blue in the clear outdoor light, as he told her whimsical tales about the Pilgrim Fathers which she knew must be purely the product of his fancy.

Before she could stop herself, Clarissa had cut off one of his stories to ask, 'And your wife, will she be as pleased to see me as Ted seems to be?'

'My wife?' His knuckles grew white on the wheel and he glanced at her incredulously. She saw a bitter look momentarily shadow his eyes and pain flash through them like a knife. Then with a grim, deliberate emphasis which made each word fall on the air like a willed reality, he said, 'My wife is dead.'

The 'I'm sorry' which flew automatically to Clarissa's lips fell on deaf ears. He was tensed in a blackness which permitted no encroachment and Clarissa shivered. A worried gnawing rose in her which his words should have put to rest.

They drove silently for a while and when he spoke again, it was in his normal tone. 'Bianca—Bianca Neri—is Jethrop's assistant marketing director, in case you were wondering. If you weren't so deliberately obtuse about everything regarding your publishers, you would have known that. Her name's on the letterhead.'

Clarissa flushed in embarrassment. 'I seem to be deliberately obtuse about a great many things, Mr Hamilton,' she said quietly, her blue eyes wide on his profile. A look passed between them and she was suddenly driven by a desire to touch him, to fold her hand over the soft grey shirt which moulded his shoulders. Instead, she looked round at Ted and gently patted the roundness of the leg folded under him.

'My name is Garrett,' the man at her side insisted, and as if in answer to her own need, he ruffled her hair, letting his hand linger on the nape of her neck for a fleeting instant. 'Say it. Garrett.'

Clarissa tried her tongue round the word, her voice slightly hoarse, tremulous.

'Difficult, isn't it?' his eyes mocked her. 'But it's better that you learn to say it now, before we have a meeting about your latest manuscript.'

'What?' Her voice broke totally now. 'Have you read it already?'

He nodded. 'All but the last few pages.'

'And?' She looked at him nervously.

'And we'll set up a meeting to talk about it some time early next week,' he said, his tone comforting her.

'But you can't just leave me dangling like that,' Clarissa blurted out. 'It's inhuman—it's vile!'

He chuckled. 'You never seem to have thought of me as human before. Why should you want me to change now?' he teased her, and then lazily he spread his fingers round her shoulder and gave her a reassuring squeeze. 'It's O.K., Clarissa. There are just a few things, but not to be discussed casually in the car.'

'Perhaps you'll decide not to promote me quite so effusively now,' she said, her teeth clenched. 'I could cheerfully go back to dignified anonymity.'

'After the spectacle you made of yourself with Adam Bennett last night?' He gave her a scathing glance. 'Don't be absurd. You've now fully registered your identity with a significant sector of the media.'

'I thought that was precisely what you wanted of me,' Clarissa sighed.

'We're here!' Ted suddenly shouted jubilantly from the back seat, and Garrett swerved the car on to a pebbled drive which led towards a hilly cluster of trees.

'Four thousand eight hundred and two, Dad. That's how many I counted!'

Clarissa turned towards the small beaming face, amazed at the child's command of numbers. 'How old are you, Ted, I never thought to ask?'

'Six going on sixteen, my dad says.' The little boy looked at her mischievously.

'Stop being a smart aleck, Ted,' Garrett commanded, and then with another turn, he drew the car up in front of a large Colonial structure. The look on Clarissa's face as she gazed at the house made him chuckle. 'My father was a builder with a flair for the grand,' he explained. 'I grew up in this house and every year— after another European escapade—the junk, now known as antiques, grew as well. As you'll see.'

'But I'm going to show Clarissa my room first,' Ted tumbled across the back seat into her lap and with one swift movement had opened the car door and was pulling her after him.

'Our English guest might think it more polite if we offered her some coffee first.' Garrett held his son back.

Clarissa shook her head. 'Ted's room sounds far more exciting.'

With a nod from his father, Ted pulled her into the house and without letting her get more than an impression of a large hall with gleaming parquet floors, he dragged her up two flights of stairs towards a room sprawling with toys, each of which—trains, robots, varieties of dinosaur and spaceship—she had to inspect with equal attention. On one of the shelves in the room she noticed a small photograph of a woman with dark waving hair holding a baby. Garrett's wife, she knew instantly. Her heart lurched oddly and she moved towards the image, but Ted drew her in another direction.

'And now for the best,' the little boy announced, pulling a large Cheshire cat down from a shelf. 'Isn't he like you? If you like him, I'll give him to you.'

'An act of amazing generosity, so you can't possibly refuse,' Garrett's rubber-soled tread had allowed him to enter the room unnoticed and now he stared down at the two figures on the floor with an easy grin lighting his face.

'But I can't have him,' Clarissa protested. 'He's too lovely—you'll miss him, Ted.'

'You must.' Ted's statement carried an irrefutable authority.

'He's a lot more persuasive than I am,' Garrett laughed, then ruffling his son's hair, he suggested that they both come for a swim.

'I haven't brought a swimming costume,' Clarissa demured.

'Bianca will lend you one. I'm sure she has a spare somewhere in the house.'

Clarissa stiffened. So Bianca lived here, whether she was Garrett's wife or not.

'Or one of Elinor's,' Ted offered. 'I know where she keeps them.' Again he dragged Clarissa after him, this time saving her an act she knew would fill her with grim distaste. Somehow the thought of wearing the sleek Bianca's clothes was particularly repellent.

'I'm sure Elinor won't mind,' Garrett reassured her explaining, 'She's the girl who looks after Ted. She's away on holiday, which is how you managed to bump into this little fellow in my office.'

Clarissa took the scanty two-piece suit Ted offered her from a bottom drawer and with a slight sense of trepidation went off to change. The house, as Garrett had suggested, was distinctly eccentric. The room to which Clarissa was taken and where she found her small bag waiting for her was an indulgent venture into Chinoiserie, or at least the Orient. An elaborately decorated blue cane bedstead, small lacquered tables and an exquisite screen with a wonderful Art Nouveau nude gently blossoming out of lavish flowers, were only some of the decorative foibles which struck Clarissa's eyes.

Garrett laughed at her expression. 'I thought you might enjoy this room particularly. We'll meet you at the pool when you're ready.' And with that, he picked Ted up and was off.

Clarissa felt she had been thrust on to a set for one of Hollywood's more extravagant movies. For a moment she forgot all her anxieties and examined the objects in the room. With a frivolous gesture she draped a frothy scarf of bright red ostrich feathers round her neck and gazed at herself in a black-lacquered body-length mirror. Then with a shiver, it occurred to her that the scarf might have belonged to Garrett's wife. She remembered the strange black moment in the car when he had said she was dead with a finality which held nothing of mourning. Reflectively, she picked up a small inlaid box, which opened magically under her fingers. Inside, it's red-cushioned lining was embroidered with the single word, *Laura*. That must have been her name, Clarissa thought, mouthing the syllables.

Quickly now, she stripped and donned the borrowed costume. She was dismayed at the way in which her rounded breasts protruded from the skimpy top. Suddenly feeling shy, she glanced at herself in the mirror. Her skin, though pale, had a tawny glow and her slight frame had its ample share of feminine curves. Uneasily, Clarissa pulled her striped tee-shirt over her shoulders, relieved to see that it reached to her thighs. The thought of Garrett's eyes on her bare skin frightened her and she reminded herself once again, 'Ted's friend.'

From a window nestled in the staircase landing, she looked out at the vista at the back of the house. Directly beneath her was a large pool, its aqua-blue waters glistening in the sunlight. Large trees bordered the area, giving it the aspect of a park, and in the midst of a cluster of trees Clarissa made out a tennis court. The sight brought a smile of pleasure to her lips and simultaneously a longing to see her brother. It was he who had taught her to play, and throughout their childhood they had engaged in matches which grew in ferocity as Clarissa's game improved.

Now she eagerly ran down the stairs and following her instincts through the house, made her way to a large room which opened on to a terrace, a few steps down from which she could see the pool. As she walked through the doors, the first sight to greet her was Bianca, resplendent in a red one-piece swimsuit which climbed high on her long legs, made even longer by a pair of high-heeled slippers.

Clarissa tried a hello which she hoped didn't sound too dreadfully brittle. In a glance the woman took in bare feet and tee-shirt and returned a disdainful, 'So Ted's little writing friend has arrived!'

Clarissa flushed with embarrassment, which only increased as she felt Garrett's eyes on her. 'Coming for a swim?' he asked, and she focussed on his lean, hard body, only to withdraw her eyes instantly.

'Quick, Clarissa!' Ted splashed a wing-clad arm from the pool and waved to her.

Steeling herself, Clarissa wriggled out of her tee-shirt and walked selfconsciously towards the pool. Garrett's eyes seemed to leave a trail on her skin, and suddenly she was distinctly angry at this man who dared gaze at her so directly, while his mistress—yes, his mistress, Clarissa repeated the word to herself, imprinting it on her mind—sat no more than eight feet away.

'Take your eyes off me!' she hissed at him.

'Why?' he arched an eyebrow in mock innocence. 'They're very happy where they are. You're not nearly so boyish as you would have us all believe,' his gaze rested mercilessly on her breasts. 'And in any case,' he chuckled, 'it's the first time I've seen you wearing a bra.'

Her cheeks flaming, Clarissa plunged into the pool, her body arcing in a clean dive which sent water spraying all over him and, she hoped, the coolly poised Bianca too. With sure swift strokes, she swam towards little Ted, who greeted her with cheers. 'You're almost as good as my dad!' he breathed excitedly.

'I heard that, you runt!' Garrett was right beside them and with a great show of pretended anger, he lunged towards his son, who splashed away from his grasp with squeals of delight.

By the time lunch was served, Clarissa had quite forgotten her early embarassment. She relished the feel of the sun on her bare shoulders. The thick slices of buttered bread and cold chicken salad tasted delicious. And if it hadn't been for Bianca's barely controlled irritation, the moment would have had a wonderful ease to it. She wondered whether Garrett and Bianca had argued about her coming to the house. It seemed strange that this evidently sophisticated woman—who talked authoritatively with Garrett about cover designs and sales figures—should treat Clarissa with such hostility. Perhaps she had wanted Garrett all to herself for the weekend; perhaps she didn't like Clarissa's book and was responsible for marketing it nonetheless . . .

The thought of her work suddenly reminded Clarissa of what Garrett had said about her manuscript. Anxiety rose in her ominously and needing to move, she interrupted the conversation around her as soon as a pause permitted.

'Anyone for tennis?'

'Do you mean I have a willing partner at last?' Garrett's broad grin gave his face an almost boyish look.

'For tennis, if nothing else,' Clarissa laughed.

Bianca rose from her chair, aggressively scraping it against the stone floor.

'You know we're supposed to be back in Manhattan by five, darling,' she said, her voice metallic.

'Oh, Dad,' Ted wailed, 'I don't want to go that early!'

The woman cut him off brusquely. 'And how do you intend to get back, Clarissa? There'll hardly be enough room for us all in the Porsche, given the luggage.' Bianca's eyes challenged her silently.

Before Clarissa had a chance to answer, Garrett

intervened. 'Oh, we'll manage. After I've run Clarissa off the tennis court, she'll be so tiny she can easily huddle into the back seat with Ted.'

Clarissa baulked. Much as she liked Ted, the thought of playing nanny to him and being patronised by Bianca, while the blonde monopolised Garrett, appealed to her not in the least. 'If you drop me at a train station, I'll make my own way back,' she said as evenly as she could, whispering to Ted, 'There'll never be enough room for Cheshire cat and me.'

A tense smile made its way on to Bianca's face.

Garrett shrugged. 'We'll settle it later. Tennis now, everyone!'

Three sets later, Clarissa was panting heavily. Garrett had beaten her easily, but it had been a good game.

As they approached each other, their eyes met over the net and Garrett gently touched her brow, lightly trailing his fingers over the curve of her cheek. Something stirred in Clarissa and she lost herself in his gaze, the crooked smile which seemed to caress her. Suddenly a troubled look clouded his features and he turned brusquely away. Clarissa stepped back, as if she had been slapped. Waves of confusion flooded through her.

His voice came after what seemed a long time. 'Shall we meet to discuss the manuscript on Monday evening?' he asked formally.

'Can't do it,' Clarissa replied, pleased that it was true, though her voice cracked over the words.

'Why not?' He sounded irritated.

'Previously engaged,' she said spitefully, and turned away.

Garrett put a restraining hand on her shoulder and held her tightly. 'Tuesday, then.'

She shook his hand off. 'If you insist. But I can't imagine that you can tell me anything about writing,' she said, desperate to hurt him for his sudden coldness.

His eyes suddenly blazed beneath the mass of white hair. 'No, perhaps not, Clarissa Harlowe. Perhaps not. But there are a few things about life I can certainly teach you!'

CHAPTER THREE

CLARISSA sat on the New York-bound train and gazed
unseeingly at the passing countryside. In retrospect she
was astounded at her behaviour over the weekend, the
way in which the various roles she had planned for
herself as mere playacting had catapulted into nothing as
soon as Garrett Hamilton entered the scene, so that she
no longer knew what came from her private core and
what was makebelieve. His presence drew gestures from
her which were simultaneously spontaneous and
unrecognisable: responses which she didn't recognise as
her own. She didn't know this woman who blew
impetuously hot and cold, who lost herself in the trance
of his eyes and then snapped uncharacteristically at a
man whose position alone should have kept her quietly
respectful.

She flushed with embarrassment as she remembered
the scene in front of the small station at which they had
dropped her: little Ted pleading with her that she drive
into New York with them; Bianca, one hand
possessively on Garrett's shoulder, thrusting barbs at
her out of icy eyes, and trying to persuade Ted that he
had had enough of his playmate for one day; Garrett
himself, standing back, a droll smile curving his lips as
he let the drama play itself out.

He had carried her bag for her to the train and with
an anger incomprehensible to herself, Clarissa had
commented, 'I don't know how you can put up with
that cow.'

'Cow?' His eyebrows rose in mock astonishment.
'She's hardly maternal enough for that. We prefer to
think of her as an ostrich. Though you shouldn't be
disrespectful to Jethrop House staff.' With that he had
chucked her under the chin as if she were Ted's size,
slammed the train door behind her and sauntered off.

Clarissa's rage had taken miles to subside, only to return as she remembered Garrett's officious counsel that she re-read her manuscript before he came to pick her up at six thirty on Tuesday evening.

But Clarissa couldn't settle to anything. Even her continuous letter to her brother went unheeded, as she found tasks for herself round the loft, walked the crowded SoHo streets and made forays into the numerous small galleries which exhibited everything from luminescent graffiti to spare bicycle tyres. She was relieved when Monday evening rolled round, and decking herself out in her new black trouser suit, she went to meet Adam Bennett at a fashionable local restaurant.

His wit and humorous flattery proved a slave. With the exuberant self-deprecation which Clarissa had learned to recognise as a particularly New York characteristic, he told her how the restaurant they were in was spectacularly expensive simply because it served as little food on each and every dish as possible. Andy Warhol had done a piece on its French owner in his *Interview* magazine and ever since then, the SoHo *gratin* had frequented it in droves.

Clarissa's ready chuckle brought more anecdotes about Warhol, how he had once announced that he was tired of autographing Campbell's soup cans and if his public had any imagination, they would get him to put his name on a lit cigarette.

'Art as the outlandish ephemeral gesture,' Clarissa breathed. 'Writing is different, isn't it?' The conversation then turned on her, and Adam suggested areas which they could cover on the TV show.

'You're very lucky to have Garrett Hamilton behind you,' he announced in the midst of things. 'He's one of the few remaining publishers to carry any weight.'

Clarissa stiffened, 'If you mean that it's his brand the media and the public are going to buy rather than my paltry contents, I'm sure you're quite right.'

He looked at her oddly. 'That's not . . .'

'Oh, drop it,' Clarissa intervened. 'I'm being

sensitive.' She hadn't really been fishing for compliments, but she was only too well aware that Garrett had suddenly become central to her life, like the puppetmaster she had once evoked, pulling the marionette's strings.

'He wouldn't push you if he didn't think your work was worth it.'

Clarissa let this pass and turned the conversation to other subjects. But the next day she forced herself to sit down with her manuscript and read it with a cool eye. There were elements in it which she knew weren't quite right and with the dread which was always the starting point for her every act of writing, she started to list some of the changes which needed to be made. Again, she wished that Garrett hadn't been allowed to see the manuscript at this stage, but she thrust his image aside and concentrated on her work. When she next looked at her watch, it was six o'clock; in a daze she scrambled into a quick shower, quickly looked through her small wardrobe, and with a sense of donning armour to meet the attack, she put on the smart little suede suit she had so recently brought.

She had just finished pulling the short skirt down over a pair of patterned tights when the buzzer rang. Pushing her feet into a pair of low pumps, Clarissa prodded the answering bell and went to open the door to wait for Garrett's progress up the stairs. She was amazed to find him already there, and she pulled back from the door.

His dark eyes flickered over her and a smile played round his lips. 'You didn't tell me which flat it was, so I had to ask the gallery people downstairs,' he explained as a greeting. He followed her into the loft and let out a low whistle. 'I didn't know your writing kept you in such style.'

Clarissa laughed nervously, taking in his presence, the dark suit which clothed him in easy elegance, the hair dramatically white against it, the strength of his face, and the eyes which seemed to her now impenetrable, masking lives she would probably never know about. With shy politeness, she showed him to the sofa and offered him some white wine, explaining at one and the same time the arrangement about the loft, the fact that she was living on the small amount of prize money she had won, and that she didn't have much to drink in the house.

He smiled at all this chatter and let his eyes wander indolently round the objects in the room, coming to rest at last on Clarissa, as she shakily poured him a glass of wine.

'The suit's a stunner,' he murmured appreciatively, and then with a playful twist of his lips, added, 'My son's right about you—a cuddly little animal, though probably a little wilder than the kind he's thinking of.'

Clarissa felt a flush rise to her cheeks. She looked at him from under thick lashes, her eyes curving delicately at the corners. Then, giving herself a mental shake, she tried a crisp voice. 'I think it would be best if we worked now. It's far more important than dinner.'

'Whatever the lady desires.' Under the lazy lids, his glance mocked her. He reached for his leather case, drew out her manuscript and patted the sofa cushion beside him, inviting her to sit by his side.

With a great show of being businesslike, Clarissa went to fetch her own copy and pulled up the armchair on the other side of the low coffee table.

Garrett let out an impatient breath and his nostrils flared slightly. Then, having congratulated her on a fine piece of writing, he proceeded to tear her novel to shreds—or so it seemed to Clarissa.

'Even though you're dealing with a fantasy world,' he told her imperiously, after having made many minor points, some of which, Clarissa acknowledged silently, as being head-on, 'your characters have to live. And while your heroine just about manages, caught up as she is in her pastoral reveries, your hero is singularly untouched by the breath of life.'

Clarissa baulked at the sententiousness of his tone. What did he know about writing? She had probably thrown away more words than he had ever conceived!

She looked at him with hatred and remembered the English quip she had heard about American publishers: big offices and small minds.

'Are you accusing me of a failure of the imagination?' she lashed out of him.

He shook his head in seeming dismay. 'You sound like a little English literature student! I'm simply suggesting that your hero had no vitality. Give him some.' Suddenly he moved towards her and in a low tone murmured, 'Like this.' With one lithe movement he pulled her out of her chair, drew her into his arms and his lips crushed down on hers with a brooding pressure, licking hers into life. Clarissa tried to pull back, but his hands caressed her back and held her to him as deftly as if he had used force. She could feel a strange new sensation kindling its way in her body so that her lips opened to his and responded as if she had been born to do nothing else. He looked deeply into her eyes, his own alight with an inner fire, and before she had time to reclaim herself, his mouth was upon hers again, bringing her arms to his neck, her hands through the tangle of his thick hair. She pressed against him, her body feeling sultry with sudden heaviness, quite unable to stand on its own. Each line of his lean shape seemed moulded against her, urging her skin into uncharted life.

Then with a gasp, she suddenly slipped away from him.

'Sex—that's all you mean! Make it sexy so that it can sell hundreds more copies!' Her high-pitched strangled voice seemed unfamiliar to her, but her eyes flashed contempt at him.

'Thousands, I hope,' he chuckled, his eyes bright beneath the heavy lids.

'Well, you can take your sex and parade it on 42nd Street!' she spat out at him, knowing she was close to tears. She had responded to his embrace with a willingness that shocked her, and she burned with humiliation and resentment, as her mind acidly told her that he had merely been engaging in a little life class.

'I rather thought I was taking you out for dinner,' his eyes trailed languorously over her. 'And stop behaving with—what did you call it when I first met you— "tremulous nobility"?—or I shall begin to think you deserve your name.' He shook his head with an air of dramatic self-contempt. 'And I don't really like to think of myself as some heartless rake.'

Speechless, Clarissa plunked herself into a chair and sat there rigidly, as if she had no intention of moving ever again.

Garrett bent over her, tousled her hair and placed a lingering kiss on her nape. She kept her body still, willing into stillness the flames that licked at her stomach.

He came round and sat opposite her. His eyes on a level with hers teased her gently. He took her hand and she let it lie in his like a stone. 'I was only trying to prove to you that more happens between a man and a woman than endless platonic dialogues.'

'The lesson is over,' she said bitterly. 'You can go now.'

'But I have no intention of going, on my own at least. And if we're to stay here, the lesson can continue.' He made to pull her towards him and with a bound, Clarissa was up and away from him.

'Ready, then?' he asked mischievously.

'You're hateful!' she breathed at him.

He chuckled. 'I shall spend the rest of the evening being so incredibly charming, you'll quite forget that I am—if I don't drop of hunger first, that is.' He reached into his briefcase and brought out several pages of handwritten script, 'And should you forget my little demonstration, Clarissa,' his eyes twinkled, 'these notes may help.'

Garrett was as good as his word. They walked the few short blocks to a restaurant in Little Italy that Clarissa had never been to before. His arm casually draped over her shoulder, he regaled her with tales of the neighbourhood's colourful and sometimes bloody history, so that by the time they had arrived she was almost oblivious to anything but his voice. Still deeply intent on a growing narrative of mean streets and moustachioed men, she ate the tortelloni and then the deliciously cooked veal placed in front of her without paying the least attention to the food. It was only when a crisp pastry stuffed with white ricotta cheese arrived that she woke to the flavour of the food and realised that she had spent the last hours so totally rapt that she had even forgotten to hate the man in front of her.

'You are charming—insidiously so,' she said to him, interrupting a sentence.

'Thank you,' he smiled at her, and offered her a cigarette. 'And you're a wonderfully talented writer, with the most seductive eyes I've encountered in a long time.'

Nervously Clarissa averted her eyes from him. Needing to move, she went in search of a loo, only to return to find his gaze travelling up her legs to the very edge of her mini.

'You realise that every man in the place has been ogling your legs for the last few minutes?' His eyes mocked her.

'Good. I shall remember to wear the same pair for the cameras,' she flung at him. 'That's what you want isn't it? A little sex thrown willy-nilly into the book. A littled added display, for your holy media. That should do the trick.'

Conflicting emotions crossed his dark face. 'Don't be cheap, Clarissa,' he said at last. 'In making you aware of yourself as a woman, I'm only suggesting to you that there are certain tensions which underline relations that, in this particular book, you've quite left out of play. It makes it flat at times. No one's telling you to introduce random sex.'

With that he rose impatiently to pay the bill. She was left looking after him, her mind going over her book and wondering whether he was perhaps right. It was, of course, not what she had been after, but perhaps by concentrating elsewhere for other effects, she had created a dull, a dead landscape. But she wouldn't give him the pleasure of letting him know he had scored a point. In any case, she concluded to herself, his tactics were appalling.

On the way back to the loft, Garrett walked so quickly that Clarissa had to all but run to keep up with him. His mind was obviously elsewhere and they exchanged hardly a word. Clarissa was beginning to regret her last outburst, but she didn't know quite what to say to him. At the steps to the loft, he turned to her and she looked up at him expectantly. His face was closed, distant, and he shook her hand almost formally, adding as something of an afterthought, 'I'd like you to finish that rewrite in about five weeks' time, if you can. Then I can take it with me to the Frankfurt Bookfair, and you as well, I think. It will help to sell it.'

Clarissa's mouth dropped open, but before she could question him, he had gone, and she was left standing on the kerb for a full minute, before she had the presence of mind to make her way slowly up the stairs.

He was, she decided firmly as she flung her clothes off and pulled on an old robe, truly appalling. Five weeks—and in that time she was supposed not only to rewrite, but do whatever publicity work cropped up. The man was mad! And then what was all this about going to Frankfurt? She knew that that was the site of the international bookfair where all the big publishing deals were made. But writers didn't often go and ... Clarissa tried to take hold of herself and think slowly, but as she lay on her bed, she was suddenly seized by the memory of Garrett's kiss, the sensation of his arms round her as they played havoc with her skin. A tremor passed through her. On the rare occasions when she had been kissed before, she had never felt anything like this. Her male acquaintances at university had always made her want to dash back to the greater pleasures of the library or her writing desk, which is where, in effect, she had spent most of her time. So that her knowledge of men had more to do with books than any actual encounters. She had, she guessed, led something of a cloistered life, though her richness of imagination had made it anything but impoverished.

Clarissa shivered again and wrapped her blanket more closely to her. And all the time that monster of a publisher had merely been teaching her a lesson, a little show of expertise to initiate her into the realm of sexual tensions. She seethed, thinking of ways in which she could get back at him.

The next day she sat down at her desk to dream her book to life. Fueled by the thought of Garrett Hamilton, and—if she dared to admit it—the subterranean life he had awakened in her, she fleshed out her characters infusing them with ambiguities. She was lost in a parallel world when, mid-afternoon, the telephone rang. It was Elizabeth's voice.

'Garrett tells me there's no need for us to meet over the manuscript, that he's already seen you. But I thought I'd just check.'

Clarissa was dying to know whether Elizabeth's views concurred with Garrett's, but not wanting to stop the flow of the book in her, she merely agreed that there was no real need for a meeting with Elizabeth. 'But he's awful, Elizabeth. I hate him,' she added.

Elizabeth chuckled. 'Now, now, hon, a little constructive criticism can't be all bad.'

'Constructive?' Clarissa yelped. 'He's got the tact of a sledgehammer!'

'But has he made you get down to it?'

'Yes,' Clarissa was forced to concur.

'Well, perhaps he thought that was the best way of handling you.'

'Manhandling me,' Clarissa murmured, and then, trying to hide her words, 'And he wants me to be finished in five weeks' time.'

'If you can, hon, it'll help. You're almost there, you know. It was a good first draft.'

'Second,' Clarissa corrected her. 'But I'll try.'

'Good,' Elizabeth consoled her, adding that she had asked Greg Lahr to try and arrange publicity work in a lump so as not to cut into Clarissa's writing time.

Clarissa worked, forgetting to eat, keeping herself going on coffee and the odd sandwich. Day and night seemed to merge into each other and sometimes when she left the house to go for a stroll, she wasn't too sure which she would encounter. The life of her book was so much stronger than the life around her that she didn't even notice which streets she was walking on. When she woke, Garrett's image suddenly confronted her senses, but she pushed it rudely out of the way and settled back at her desk.

One day, the telephone startled her out of her reverie and his voice, instantly recognisable, entered her consciousness.

'Just ringing to see how you're getting on.'

'Fine,' Clarissa answered vaguely.

'I've also got an invitation for you from Ted. He wants to know if you'll join him in the country this weekend.'

'Him?' Clarissa queried the careful phrasing.

'Yes, I have to go off to Chicago.'

'Tell him I'd love to, but since his dad has given me a deadline, I can't budge from my desk.' With that she banged the phone down, feeling somehow insulted that it should be the son rather than the father who should occasion an invitation. Chicago, she thought venomously; and probably with that Bianca of his!

Clarissa tried to settle back to her book, but Garrett's voice had broken her momentum, and instead she indulged herself by writing a long letter to her brother, something she hadn't done for days. Then, suddenly restless, she ventured out for a walk, wandered into a coffee shop and treated herself to a gigantic sandwich and a large piece of creamy cheesecake. Still restless, she roamed through the open-air fairground with its large ferris wheel and colourful market stalls, before at last heading back for home.

She padded up the stairs in her soft-soled shoes, and stopped in momentary surprise as she found her door a few inches open. She was certain that she had locked it as usual. She then noted, in some confusion, that the lock looked as if it had been broken. Suddenly frightened, she opened the door, to see in the eerie light of the street lamp a stranger rifling through drawers, the papers on her desk scattered on the floor. Panic surged in her and the scream that rose in her throat wouldn't emerge. She saw the man coming towards her and she turned to run, but a heavy thud on the back of her neck made her crumple into oblivion.

Clarissa woke to consciousness to find herself stretched out on the sofa, a large black man by her side holding her wrist. As the mists in her head cleared, another face appeared. Garrett Hamilton, his brow furrowed in worry, looked down on her and mouthed a 'Hello, welcome back among the living.'

She lost herself in his eyes and then slowly remembered coming home, the burglar. How had Garrett come into the picture?

'I found you sprawled on the floor when I came round,' he seemed to read her mind. 'I thought after you so unceremoniously hung up on me that I'd better check to see how you were getting on.' He chuckled, but his eyes were dark with concern. 'Lucky you made me so angry.'

Clarissa tried to get up, but the stranger at her side gently pushed her back. 'Not just yet, young lady. I want to check your blood pressure first.'

'Listen to the doctor, Clarissa,' Garrett chided her. 'And save your energy for the police. They'll be round in a moment.'

Clarissa's eyes grew round in fear. 'Has a lot been stolen?' her voice croaked out of her.

'It's hard to tell from my initial look around,' Garrett replied. 'I think you probably scared them away. There's more of a mess than anything else.'

'Oh, God!' Clarissa moaned. 'And it's not my place.'

'Don't worry, young lady,' the doctor consoled her. 'New Yorkers always have ample insurance.'

'How do I . . .'

'Stop worrying, Clarissa,' Garrett's voice was stern. 'I'll take care of things.'

'Yes, look after your horse. Make sure the publisher's stable doesn't suffer,' she whipped back at him. Her words, the bitterness of her tone, surprised her, and instantly she regretted them. Clarissa stretched out a hand to him. He clasped it and held it gently, stroking her fingers until a warmth crept over her whole body.

'Well, I think you'll live, young lady—though you may feel a bit stiff and headachy for a few days. He must have given you a good clean judo chop.' The doctor smiled a toothy smile at her and packed his implements back into his bag. 'A little coffee and whisky wouldn't do any harm—get the blood circulating.'

Clarissa felt her blood was circulating quite well enough, thanks to the pressure of Garrett's hand, but letting her go, he went to prepare the doctor's remedy. She sat up, a dull throbing at the back of her neck accompanying her movement, and looked round in a daze. The flat seemed to be in chaos. With a strangled sob, she got up, feeling she must put some order in the place.

Garrett stopped her movement, well aware of the object of her concern. 'Perhaps you should let the stable boy see to the clearing up. Frisky young colts who've suffered a fall need looking after,' his eyes mocked her gently.

Clarissa gave him an odd look and then subsided meekly into the sofa and sipped her toddy. When the police arrived, she answered their questions tersely, describing the man she had seen as best she could, but letting Garrett fill in official details. She was suddenly overwhelmingly grateful for his presence. She didn't think she could have borne these two gum-chewing, gun-toating, loutish men who were walking parodies of movie cops; while Garrett, with his natural authority, made short shrift of their questions and sent them packing. After the doctor had had a few quick words with Garrett, he too left.

Tears now poured down Clarissa's cheeks and however hard she tried, she couldn't stop them. Garrett was instantly beside her and gently putting an arm round her, he drew her to him so that she nestled against him, taking comfort from his solidity.

'It's the shock,' he whispered into her hair, ruffling it tenderly. 'You've had two strong doses of life in rapid succession!'

She raised tear-filled eyes to him to see whether he was laughing at her, but his look was mellow, and with infinite care he wiped the tears from her face and kissed her softly, his cool lips lingering on her cheeks. Too distraught to consider the significance of her gesture, Clarissa snuggled against him. A look of surprise winged across his face, followed by what seemed like a mute ache, and then his lips were on hers, their touch featherlight. Her arms drew round him, caressing his strong back, the crisp edges of his hair, and she opened her mouth to him, feeding on the growing intensity of his kiss. Suddenly his hands were cupping her face, gently, urgently withdrawing it from his. He looked deeply into her eyes, his own black with seriousness. Then his lips curved into a sad smile.

'Not now, little one,' he squeezed her shoulder. 'I would be taking unfair advantage of you, of us both.'

Abruptly he stood to his full height, loosened his tie, and with an irritated gesture switched on the television set.

'You're not going to leave me here alone, are you?' Clarissa's voice squeaked out of her as a trembling seized her limbs.

'No, silly,' he was immediately at her side, his arms round her. 'In fact I was going to take you home with me, but the doctor suggested it would be better if you took it easy for a few days and ...' he looked at her intently, 'and didn't develop a panic about this place. It's only part of one's initiation into New York life,' he smiled down at her crookedly. 'So I've arranged to stay here with you.'

Clarissa realised she should feel as much panic about his staying as about his going, but she was relieved and again she snuggled against him, focussing her eyes a little fuzzily on the screen.

The next thing she knew she was lying on her bed,
bright sunlight pouring through the slats of the high-
perched window of the gallery room. She opened her
eyes a little dazedly, trying to think why she felt distinctly odd, and she suddenly remembered. Instantly, too,
she realised that she was quite naked under her blankets
and that she couldn't recall having readied herself for
bed. A hot flush spread over her. Garrett! Her cheeks
burned. Where was he now? Where had he slept?

Clarissa searched under her pillow and finding the
white Victorian nightie in its habitual place, she slipped
it on and padded down the stairs.

'Hi,' a cheerful voice reached her from the kitchen
area. 'I'm Elinor. I dropped Ted at school and came
round so that Garrett could go off to work.'

Clarissa saw a dark pretty girl of no more than
eighteen sipping a cup of coffee. Her curly dark hair
flounced round a madonna-like face and her jet black
eyes inspected Clarissa with wary wisdom. She must
have decided the slight figure in the long white nightie
was all right, because a wide smile filled her face.
'I've made you some bacon and eggs and some tea.
Garrett told me you were English.' She flew round
the kitchen and piled a plate high with food. 'I'm
Puerto Rican.'

Clarissa smiled shyly back at the girl and sat down at
the small kitchen table. Miraculously, the loft seemed to
have been returned to order. Garrett must have worked
all night.

'Are you feeling all right?' Elinor asked.

Clarissa nodded.

'Well, now you've had your proper welcome to New
York. I can tell you, you're lucky not to have had your
face bashed in. See this?' Elinor pointed to her
glistening teeth. 'Only one row of them is real. The
others . . .' she aimed a fist at her own cheek.

Before Clarissa had finished sipping her second cup
of tea, she had heard the dreadful list of Elinor's
misadventures—her drunken father, thug of a brother,
how Garrett had saved her two years ago from her

family, her terrible boy-friend and from certain drug
addiction. Clarissa thought she might be listening to a
newsreel on the horrors of New York, but she knew
that despite Elinor's quick smile and ready wit, her
story was undoubtedly true, and she gazed at the girl's
youthful face with something akin to awe.

'Garrett is wonderful, isn't he? A rare gentlemen.'

Clarissa nodded her assent, not trusting her voice.

'He warned me that I shouldn't talk too much and let
you rest,' Elinor added, giggling a little.

Clarissa demured, but the girl got up nonetheless. 'I'll
just do these dishes, while you get on with things. I can
run a bath for you. O.K.?'

Clarissa smiled, pleading that she was quite capable
of doing that for herself, and she proceeded to do so,
wondering all the while at Elinor's good humour, while
she, fortunate mortal that she was, moped around
worrying about silly things like the writing of books
and their publishers. She scowled at her own
selfishness.

By the time she emerged from a long lazy bath,
Clarissa felt quite refreshed. Elinor was stretched out on
the sofa reading a book and she greeted her with a,
'Better now?'

Clarissa nodded.

'Hey, this book of yours is terrific! I'm really
enjoying it.'

Clarissa noticed that the book in front of Elinor was
her own and she blushed. 'I'm so glad.'

'Ya, it's really good.' Elinor waved a small hand at
her and re-immersed herself in the volume.'

With a sudden burst of energy, Clarissa began to
look round the flat to see if anything of note had
disappeared. She knew she had to make out a complete
list for the police. The silver seemed to be in place, as
were the stereo and the television, that much she had
noted yesterday evening. Carefully she looked at the
collection of jade and alabaster figurines. Yes, one of
these, perhaps two, were distinctly missing. Odd, she
thought, an English thief would have been less selective,

taken them all. A shudder passed through her as she remembered the man she had glimpsed in the half light. But she perisisted in her inspection. The cluster of Russian icons was, thankgoodness, all still in its corner, but as she moved towards her writing desk, a wave of hysteria rose in her. Her manuscript! She had left it scattered on the top of her desk. Distraught, Clarissa rifled through the drawers. Perhaps Garrett had tidied it away. No, it was gone. Some of her notes, her diary, were still there, but the manuscript was nowhere in sight. A cry broke from her lips.

'What is it, Clarissa?' Elinor hurried to her side.

Clarissa stared at her in momentary non-recognition and then, her lips dry, she mouthed, 'My manuscript! I think it's been stolen!'

'Oh, my God!' Elinor clutched her hands to her head. 'Have you looked everywhere?'

Clarissa nodded and then started her search again, frantically going through the loft. At last she slumped on to the sofa, her head throbbing in pain.

'Garrett must have a copy. I'll phone him right now.' Elinor lifted the receiver.

'But not the copy I was working on, Elinor,' the tears sprang to Clarissa's eyes, 'the revised one. I'll never finish in time for Frankfurt now!'

Elinor patted her shoulder and handed her the telephone. 'He's there,' she mouthed.

Making an effort to keep her voice from rising into incomprehensible shrillness, Clarissa spoke to Garrett.

'I don't know why anyone should want a scrawly manuscript,' she repeated over and over. 'Except me. And nothing else is gone except for two jade figurines.'

There was a pause at the other end of the telephone. 'It is odd,' Garrett said reflectively. 'But try to keep calm, Clarissa. I'll have a copy with you in an hour. I'll bring it myself.'

Clarissa sat staring fixedly into space until Garrett arrived.

'It's no good,' she said to him in a lifeless voice. 'I'll never be able to reconstruct all those changes in time for your deadline. And your notes—they're all gone too. Why would anyone take them?'

He shrugged and tried a joke. 'Perhaps you've got secret admirers. A network of university library manuscript thieves who've sniffed out that you're going to be worth collecting.'

Clarissa looked at him blankly, unable to laugh.

He squeezed her shoulder reassuringly. 'Give it a try, Clarissa. If you don't make the deadline—well, too bad.' He looked seriously into her eyes. 'But if by some miracle, you can manage it, that would be wonderful. I'll give you all the help I can; re-do the notes, provide a typist, give you another practical demonstration,' his voice teased her, and as the sense of his words came home to her, Clarissa flushed hotly.

'That won't be necessary,' she mumbled.

He gave her a light kiss. 'I've got to get back for a meeting now. Elinor will look after you for as long as you like. And I'll get an approximation of those notes to you by this evening.' He squeezed her shoulder again, and after a brief exchange with Elinor, he was off.

Clarissa sat numbly staring at the heap of papers in front of her.

Elinor handed her a cup of coffee and looked at her mournfully. 'I know how you feel,' she said. 'You just want to give up. I felt like that the last time my boyfriend beat me up and stole my savings.'

Clarissa gazed at the pretty young girl at her side and shook herself mentally. How could she sit here wallowing in self-pity over a mere stream of words when Elinor . . .

With sudden alacrity, Clarissa stood up and kissed Elinor on both cheeks. 'Right, mate, it's off to the grindstone! And stop looking after me so well—I feel like a spoiled brat!'

The girl flashed her a luminous smile, and straightening her shoulders, Clarissa went to her desk to try to settle to work.

Good as his word, Garrett delivered pages full of

notes to her that evening, but after a brief pep talk he left, saying he had to get back to Ted. The next day he came round with the little boy for a short visit. Concerned as he seemed about her work, polite in his enquiries after her health, she realised after he had gone that there had been a distinct lack of anything else—no mark of that special attention which she thought she had read in his eyes on the night of the burglary.

Over the platefuls of spicy food which Elinor had prepared for their dinner, she asked the girl,

'What was Garrett's wife like?'

Elinor shrugged. 'I don't know. I never met her. He never talks about her.'

Clarissa wanted then to ask about his relationship with Bianca, but she bit the words off her tongue. It was hardly a tactful subject to raise, even with a young girl as obviously worldly as Elinor.

'Garrett's very generous, very good at helping, but he's very secretive,' the girl offered of her own accord, and sighed, leaving Clarissa in no doubt that she thought him the best man in the world.

As the next days passed and the painful aching in her neck and head ceased, Clarissa's life fell into an almost military discipline. She worked at her desk until she could feel her eyes closing; then she showered and climbed into bed. It was only here that her thoughts strayed away from her book and returned with abominable regularity to Garrett. He phoned her frequently, kindly enquiring about her health and progress—but he didn't come to see her. And for some reason, as she lay there too wound up to sleep after a long day tensed at her desk, Clarissa grew distinctly angry with him. Feeding on itself during the long nights, the anger fanned itself into a burning rage. How dared that man tamper with her feelings, toy with her body, only to teach her something which she could make into material for her work? She seethed quietly, waking in the mornings to distil her anger into the words of her book.

She was surprised several days after the burglary to

receive a phone call from Bianca. 'I do hope you're not taking it too hard.' The woman seemed genuinely to be commiserating with her, and with a pang of guilt, Clarissa promised herself that she would have to revise her opinion of her.

'And the revision? Will you get it done in time for Frankfurt?' Bianca asked.

'It seems unlikely, but I'm trying,' Clarissa answered.

'Well, never mind,' Bianca consoled her. 'I've got my people working on *Children of Summer*. The second book can wait.'

Clarissa thanked her for ringing. As she was about to hang up, she heard a man's voice dimly in the background. Garrett, she thought at once, and despite her promise to herself that she would nurture kinder feelings towards Bianca, a wave of pure hostility surged through her.

One evening Elinor announced that if Clarissa was really better, she should get back to Ted. 'Garrett doesn't complain. But I know he finds it hard to manage and the arrangements for picking him up from school get hopelessly complicated,' the girl explained.

'Of course you must go,' Clarissa concurred. 'You've been an angel, an absolute dear,' she hugged the girl of whom she had indeed grown very fond. 'But you must come back and visit and I'll cook for you for a change—a complete English meal.'

'Terrific!' Elinor beamed. 'And I'll drop in to see you with Ted. He's madly in love with you.'

Unlike his rotter of a father, Clarissa said to herself, then stilled the tide of resentment that swept through her. Very soon she was to begin on her round of interviews, and it would be far better to start those on an even keel.

CHAPTER FOUR

CLARISSA watched nervously as the make-up girl applied layer after layer of shadow to her eyelids, blending browns and pinks and soft greens into a true impressionistic haze. Over the foundation had come blusher and highlights, and then oodles of mascara, until Clarissa thought her lids would be too heavy to move. And as a finishing touch, lip liner and a soft brown lustre. She looked at her new face in astonishment. Its sophistication stared at her like a mask, strange yet familiar.

'You're a natural,' the make-up girl told her, and when Clarissa turned to Greg Lahr, who sat reading a magazine in the corner, all he did was a utter a low, 'You'll wow them!'

True to her threat to Garrett Hamilton, Clarissa had worn her new mini for her television debut, and now as she walked towards the studio to meet Adam Bennett, she tried to pull the short skirt further down her legs. 'You're mad,' she told herself, 'letting that man provoke you into inanities.'

But Adam Bennett was, if nothing else, an expert at making people feel at ease in front of harsh lights and cameras. He engaged Clarissa in conversation, first of all exactly along the lines they had mapped out together. Then, when she had finished relaying the stories she had concocted for herself about her childhood—which approximated the truth, she assured herself—he drew her out on other subjects, leading her on with half-truths about literature and about England, which he knew would provoke her to sometimes heated response. By the time the other guests had joined them, the pert, slightly eccentric persona of an English writer Clarissa had rehearsed for herself was in full swing and witticisms flew across the studio set.

The programme over, Adam embraced her heartily. 'You were brilliant!' he said, and Clarissa, who had grown used to American overstatement, decided that she had probably not made too great a ninny of herself. She refused his invitation to dinner that night, pleading that by that time she would be utterly exhausted. In any case, she admitted to him, she wanted to watch the programme which would be broadcast that evening in blissful isolation, 'just in case I find myself in tears.' But she promised to see him later that week.

Greg chaperoned her through the afternoon's schedule of radio interviews and left her at her door. She looked at it with momentary panic and then, forcing herself, she walked up the stairs, checked that her own door was soundly locked, and went in. She was totally drained. After a hot bath, she lay down on her bed for what she thought would be a brief rest, only to wake at midnight and discover that she had missed her television debut. She giggled, thinking that it was probably a kind fate which had ordained her falling asleep.

Padding down the stairs, she fixed herself a quick snack, then glanced at her writing desk. There were only a few days left until the publishing monster's deadline was at hand, and Clarissa had promised herself that even if she grew ill in the process, she would meet it. Two chapters still needed fixing up and she wanted to revamp the opening. With a sigh, she sat down and forced herself to recapture the thread. How much more possible it all would have seemed if the revision she had originally started on had not been mysteriously stolen!

The next morning the telephone woke her from sleep and she let it ring itself out, unable to drag herself out of bed. Then when it started again a few minutes later, she glanced at her watch, to find that it registered eleven o'clock. She groaned. It was time to get up, and she trekked slowly down the narrow staircase to the telephone. Greg's excited voice wiped the last traces of sleep from her mind, 'I've had at least four phone calls about you already this morning, Clarissa, and—wait for it, one of them from Gordon Foster!'

Clarissa's mind blanked, 'Who?' she queried.

'Gordon Foster. You must know—it's the network talk show. It goes out nationwide at prime time, every night.'

'And so?' Clarissa stared bleakly at the telephone, wanting nothing more than to go back to bed.

'So, it's wonderful!' She could hear Greg's dismay at his unshared excitement. 'I said I'd just check with you to see whether you were free to do it on Thursday night.'

'Why not,' said Clarissa, 'as long as I have most of Wednesday to myself, as you promised.'

Greg chuckled. 'Yes, but I'm going to work you to death on the other days. Pick you up at one, O.K.?'

'Yes,' Clarissa answered, and rang off. She brewed herself some coffee, but before she had a chance to drink any of it the telephone rang again. It was Elizabeth this time, congratulating her on the programme. 'You were wonderful,' she chortled. 'I could have kissed you! You coped beautifully.'

'Did I?' Clarissa laughed. 'Don't tell anyone, Elizabeth, but I slept through the programme. Was it really all right?'

'Blissful! You're a mad girl,' Elizabeth giggled, adding, 'And don't forget the launch party here on Friday. The hordes will be gathering to meet their find of the month.'

'Don't worry, I'll be there, trailing clouds of glory,' Clarissa mocked herself.

Elizabeth's call was followed by another from Elinor, and only when she had rung off did Clarissa sit down again to finish her coffee. With a sudden wave of irritation she realised that the only person who hadn't rung to congratulate her was Garrett. Simply couldn't be bothered, she said to herself, hating him momentarily.

Too jittery to return to her manuscript in the time left her before Greg's arrival, she decided on a walk instead.

It would calm her, and this interviewing was proving hard work, much harder than she had imagined.

By the end of that day's list, she felt she couldn't face another interested face, another question. Greg tried to cheer her on.

'You're lucky it's only pre-publicity we're doing. If the book were already out, you'd be faced by the women's groups as well—hordes of serious faces asking you intense questions.'

'God preserve me!' Clarissa bleated. 'I'd go into hiding. You know, Greg, the truth is, I'm just a writer. I have nothing to say when I'm talking to people, or at least no more than anyone else.'

He smiled at her as if she had just made the most preposterous of statements.

The next day was her day off, and Clarissa sat at her desk determined to finish the revision on her manuscript. She was now furious at Garrett, the fact that he hadn't made a sign all week. 'I'm going to throw this manuscript in his face when it's done,' she promised herself, and with a vengeance she started to work.

By the time Thursday evening rolled round and she sat once again in a make-up chair, she knew she was paralytic with fatigue and that the make-up girl had to work doubly hard to hide the shadows under her eyes. Probably better this way, she thought. She was too tired to be nervous and she had even let Greg help her choose a dress suitable for the occasion. These late night shows meant glitter and lamé, and Clarissa felt there was nothing more unlike her, so she had insisted that they hire something, rather than squander money uselessly. As it was, she found herself in a long black sequined contraption which left one shoulder bare, ended in a sequined clasp on the other, and smoothly moulded her shape. Greg had insisted it was a stunner. He had even used the word 'elegant'. But Clarissa felt like a vamp decked out for an evening at the Ritz, and her eyes, larger than life, stared back at her unfamiliarly from the mirror.

But nothing had prepared her for the ordeal of the

Gordon Foster Show, which she hadn't yet deigned to watch. He was a smooth unctuous character with wavy black hair, and Clarissa took an instant dislike to him, which only deepened as he tried to win her over with comments, the silliness of which offended her. Her initial trepidation when she had walked on-stage to realise that this time she was to be faced by a live audience disappeared into unparalleled contempt for the man next to her. And when—after he had asked her to recount what her book was about, to which she answered by rote and at length, trying to keep her voice lively—he asked her what there was in it which she thought would interest Americans, she said bluntly, 'I have no idea. You might ask my publishers. They're American and they seem to think they're human, like the rest of us.'

There was a roar of laughter from the audience and Gordon Foster prodded her. 'But there must be something special, otherwise they'd simply publish you and forget about you. Your book would be remaindered almost before it reached the shops. Why are they promoting you?'

Clarissa gazed at him as if he were an impertinent flea. 'I haven't the foggiest,' she answered blankly. 'I guess they want to make some money, some profit. That's what it's all about, isn't it? You might ask one of them—Garrett Hamilton, for instance.'

'So you don't approve of making money? You're a labourite, perhaps? A socialist?'

The man was totally ridiculous, Clarissa thought. What on earth had his present question to do with what she had said, except on the most simple-minded level? And before she quite knew what she was saying, she uttered, 'Aren't you, Mr Foster? Aren't all sensible people at least some time in their lives?' She turned innocent eyes on him. The audience was in uproar and the smile on Gordan Foster's face grew so glassy that Clarissa thought it must shatter in a hundred pieces.

Greg drove her home that night with the exclamation that the programme would make the book sell millions, but he seemed to be looking at her with something akin to fright and Clarissa was too tired to reassure him. She fell asleep almost as soon as her head touched her pillow, only to wake with a dreadful sense of impending anxiety. Oh yes, today was the day she absolutely had to finish her revision, and bleary-eyed, she trudged to her desk, taking the phone off the hook on the way. It was now only a question of rereading the whole and putting in the finishing touches.

By four o'clock, she wearily turned the last page. Then she took herself off for a long soak and a nap, setting her alarm, this time for six. She was due at the launch party at seven-thirty and she had toyed with ringing up Garrett's secretary to ask if she could see him just before that so that she could fling the manuscript in his face. But she had decided against it. She would take him by surprise.

She dressed carefully in her black trouser suit, her freshly washed hair gleaming on her head, her eyes suddenly taking on a sparkle as she thought vengefully of the look on Garrett's face when she confronted him. Then she went downstairs, hailed a cab and found herself in the awesome headquarters of Jethrop House at ten past seven.

She took the lift up to Garrett's floor, suddenly distinctly aware of every moment of their first meeting, her astonishment when that white head had revealed a youthful face, the drama of his gaze, his hateful arrogance. She shivered, then with an angry bounce in her step, made her way to his office, pressing the buzzer on the outer door which bore his name, hearing his voice, identifying herself and then pushing open his door without so much as a knock.

'Here it is!' she announced loudly, flashing the package even before she had fully opened the door.

But he sight that confronted her stopped her in her tracks. Bianca Neri, in a clinging mauve satin dress, stood with her arms round Garrett, her face raised to his in a kiss. Garrett's eyes turned on Clarissa, but before he could speak she had lashed out, 'The bloody revision you wanted—well, there it is!' She dropped it on the floor and slammed the door behind her.

She raced along the corridor back to the lift, and only then stopped to catch her breath. Tears bit at her eyes. The humiliation of it! she gasped to herself. Not even the decency to step out of his mistress's arms when he knows I'm coming in. She poured scorn on herself for her own stupidity and with a helpless look round her searched for a loo into which she could disappear. She couldn't face a crowd of people now, not for the good of any book.

But none of the doors that faced her provided any respite, and with a shrug, she jabbed at the lift button again. She would go up to the penthouse where the launch party was taking place. It would serve Jethrop's right if their writer of the month walked in with streaming eyes and a red nose, dishevelled to the point of idiocy. Garrett would undoubtedly think it made good copy for the scandalmongers and any publicity was, as the odious media crew would have it, good publicity.

When she had emerged from the lift, Clarissa instantly saw a women's room, and a little of her native good sense taking over, she went into it to try and assemble herself a little. Tear-filled eyes in a stricken face gazed out at her from the mirror, and the sight of her own misery made her pause and take stock of herself. Had her feelings for that abominable man reached such a point that the sight of him with the woman whom she knew all too clearly took precedence over her could reduce her to pulp? She felt like throwing something at her own stupid reflection: she was behaving like some ninny of a Victorian parlourmaid in the throes of puppy love for her distant employer, who had chanced surreptitiously to pinch her rump on a number of occasions or sneak a kiss in the broom closet. Never would Garrett catch a glimpse of the way in which she had let her emotions run away with her, Clarissa resolved. Monster that he was, with his piercing intelligence, his writers, his mistresses, his wife, forgotten by the looks of it before she was even cold—Clarissa's catalogue soared into hysterical heights.

Steeling herself, she washed her face and applied some fresh make-up.

'Hello, you famous television personality!' Elizabeth's smiling face suddenly appeared in the mirror behind her and then furrowed in concern as it gazed at Clarissa's reflection. 'Is something wrong, hon?'

Clarissa shook her head. 'Just exhaustion. I've finished the revision,' she offered by way of explanation.

Elizabeth hugged her. 'You've been angelically uncomplaining—and,' her blue eyes twinkled, 'the sales people tell me the phones have been buzzing with orders all day. Thanks, no doubt, to your performance with Gordon Foster last night. I don't know whether you intended to, but you put him down royally. It'll make you some enemies,' she added noncommittally after a moment.

Clarissa shrugged. 'He was just so . . .'

'Awful!' the two women said in unison, then laughed.

'Come on,' Elizabeth dragged Clarissa along with her, 'one more evening's effort and then you're free.'

'To wait for the reviews,' Clarissa commented morosely. 'When they appeared in England, I locked myself in my room for a week—and then I had my brother to hold my hand. Now . . .'

'Now I'll hold your hand and feed you on chicken soup to boot,' Elizabeth reassured her. 'Anyhow, there's no reason for you to read them if it upsets you. Half of my writers don't bother. They just rely on friends to tell them the good things.'

'I don't think I'm quite cool enough for that yet,' Clarissa looked bleak. 'Perhaps after another few books.'

The two women strolled into the penthouse already crowded with people. Clarissa looked round her in amazement. The room, glazed on three sides, looked out on the glittering spires of Manhattan and its curling rivers, midnight blue in the dying light. A terrace planted with small shrubs and trees surrounded the space, and here guests had also gathered. Clarissa wanted nothing more than to proceed to the terrace alone and delight in the magic twilight of the city, but she was stopped halfway there by an excited Adam Bennett, who tailed after her when she exclaimed that she simply had to get her tourist's eyeful of the vista before night descended.

Once they were outdoors, he threw his arms around her euphorically and planted a moist kiss on her lips. Then, his arms still round her, he looked into her eyes and slowly announced, 'Clarissa, you're magnificent!'

Clarissa looked at him questioningly, too surprised to wriggle out of his grip.

'Last night,' he explained in response to her look. 'With Gordon Foster. You were out of this world! I've been thinking, scheming all night. How would you like to share the next season of my shows with me? It would be terrific.'

'I think Clarissa would prefer to continue writing. And given that she keeps to deadlines so well, I think her talent should be encouraged,' a deep voice rumbled behind her, and Garrett Hamilton came into view, his whole rugged demeanour speaking of barely controlled rage. 'Would you leave us for a moment, Adam,' he said. 'Clarissa and I have a few details to discuss privately.'

Adam Bennett was not to be so lightly got rid of, and with just a slight shrug of his shoulders and a complicitous look at Clarissa, he kissed her full on the lips again. 'We'll talk it over at dinner.' And before Clarissa had a chance to reply, he ambled away.

'Aren't you taking this business of promotion a little too seriously?' Garrett's dark eyes cut into her.

'Director's orders,' Clarissa thrust at him, 'and I've taken your advice about exploring subterranean tensions between men and women as well.' She turned on her heel, unable to face his proximity.

A biting grip on her shoulder stopped her. 'And what

was the idea of referring to me in that way on the programme last night, Clarissa?' he hissed out her name between clenched lips. 'I've had the board breathing down my neck all day!'

'Serves you bloody well right!' she lashed out at him, turning to face him. 'It was all your doing.'

'My doing?' he breathed heavily, and glared at her. 'I would never have let you appear on Foster's programme if I'd known about it. He's a fool, despite his friends in high places.'

'Didn't you know?' Clarissa looked at him disbelievingly.

'Of course not,' he barked at her. 'I've been away most of the week. Don't you think I would have been in touch if I hadn't? And I've been trying to ring you on and off all day, but your line was continually engaged.' The exasperation was clear in his strong face.

Clarissa eyed him suspiciously. She wanted to believe him, but the memory of Bianca entwined in his arms made her stubbornly resistant. 'It's all your doing, in any case,' she muttered. 'You got me involved in all this promotional business.'

He looked, she thought, as if he wanted to do nothing more than smack her and suddenly afraid, she made to walk away. But once again he gripped her, his fingers eating into her arm and guided her indoors where the crowd had grown.

'Since you've learned so much about this matter of self-promotion, let's see if you can charm the chairman of the board with those seductive eyes of yours,' he growled. 'He needs some pacifying.'

Clarissa shook her arm free of his and turned wide caressing eyes up at him, a playful smile hovering round her lips, 'Will that do?'

'Beautifully,' he scowled at her, and then, his face relaxing, he laughed a low, mellow sound. 'Beautifully. You look all of sixteen.'

'And never been kissed,' Clarissa finished for him, her blue eyes gazing provocatively into his.

'But we know better than that,' a vulnerable

expression flitted across his face and Clarissa suddenly
ached to touch him. But it was gone as soon as it had
come, to be replaced by a confident formality. 'Mr
Hargreaves, may I introduce Clarissa Harlowe; Clarissa,
the chairman of Jethrop House.'

Clarissa went through her paces, performing, she felt,
like a well-trained animal, mollifying the old man,
telling him how nervous she had been the previous
evening so that she had babbled out anything that had
come into her mind.

'Well, you've got him eating out of your hand,'
Garrett murmured as he led her away. 'Is there anyone
else you'd like to take on?' The acid tone of his words
provoked her.

She let her eyes roam the room coolly. 'How about
that exquisite black man over there? Is he important
enough for me to talk to? Will it sell any books?'

'Bitch.' He met her eyes momentarily, his own
gleaming darkly, and casually manouevred her towards
her desired end, then promptly abandoned her.

Clarissa sighed wearily. This whole evening was
becoming more than she could bear. She let herself be
dragged by Elizabeth or Greg Lahr from conversation
to conversation, saying little, and was almost relieved
when Adam Bennett asked her if she was ready to be
kidnapped away to a succulent dinner.

Clarissa nodded. From somewhere across the room,
she could feel Garrett's eyes on her, but he made no
attempt to say goodnight. Adam's enthusiastic description of their possible mutual venture—which he detailed
grandly throughout dinner—did nothing to lift her
spirits. It was no good protesting to him that she was
not a public person, that she was desperately shy and
only happy at her desk, when these last days she had,
by whatever magic of adrenalin or personality, shown
herself to be something quite other as well. So she
promised Adam that she would think about his
proposal. But at the moment all her thoughts centred
on a warm bed and a good book. And, though she
didn't say it aloud, on Garrett Hamilton. She didn't

much like the woman she had become in this last while, battling words coming easily from her mouth, words which shielded her as much or more than they expressed what she felt. And she couldn't blame Garrett much if he didn't like her either.

She woke the next morning, her mouth dry with tension, her throat constricted. She felt balefully depleted, as if she had used up all her reserves of energy on revising her manuscript, on rushing about from interview to interview, now only to be left alone, emptied out, like a fountain which had ceased to flow. And on top of it all, her mind *would* keep returning, awake or asleep, to the image of Garrett caught in an embrace with Bianca. It was all too clear to her after the previous evening's events that although Garrett might be the first man ever to have made any real impact on her, he was also totally beyond her reach— unless she wanted to be caught in a triangle which spelled trouble in large letters.

She tossed in her bed, willing sleep to descend on her again. But it was useless. She might as well get up. Perhaps a little tourist adventure would refresh her—a trip to the Statue of Liberty. She had kept well away from it before, thinking that it was really too conventional a thing to be doing. But today, why not? She urged herself into the shower, letting the prickly stream of water massage her body back into life. When she had finished shampooing her hair, the telephone rang, and impatiently she sloshed out of the shower to pick it up.

'No protests. We'll be round in half an hour to pick you up,' Garrett's voice commanded over the wires, and he had hung up before Clarissa had quite assimilated who was going to pick her up and what for.

Under the impetus of the order, she dried herself hurriedly, pulled on a pair of white trousers and a sparkling white shirt. No sooner had she finished buttoning it then there was another ring, this time the doorbell. It's never half an hour, Clarissa thought to herself, and was about to shout down the ansaphone that Garrett would have to wait, when Adam Bennett identified himself, insisting that he had to come up and give her something.

Muttering about these imperious Americans, Clarissa opened the door to him. His clever eyes sparkled as with one hand he presented her with a bag of croissants, and with the other waved a sheaf of papers.

'The first two reviews are wonderful!' he announced gleefully.

Clarissa felt a nervous anxiety tighten her stomach. 'I'll make some coffee,' she said, working to keep her voice calm. 'I don't want to look at the reviews now.' Having one's work reviewed was quite enough like having one's soul dissected in public, without the added strain of a stranger waiting for one's response to the dissection.

Adam gazed at her questioningly, then with a shrug put the papers to one side and pulled up a chair at the kitchen table. With deliberate motions, Clarissa prepared the coffee, and when she had placed a mug in front of Adam, he passed her a few pages of typescript.

'I got so enthusiastic last night about our doing a joint show that I put some ideas down on paper.' His mouth crinkled into a smile.

Clarissa looked cursorily at the list of subjects he had sketched. Some instantly caught her interest, and she admitted as much to Adam, adding that fascinating as the proposal might be, she couldn't see herself doing it. 'In any case, I have no idea whether I'll still be here next year,' she looked at him seriously. 'My sub-let runs out in a couple of months, and I think I've probably had enough of New York.'

'Nonsense,' he argued with her. 'You haven't so much as scratched the surface of this town yet.'

Clarissa admitted it all too readily, but that, she pointed out, didn't change her apprehension about too much time off from writing—even though the money would come in more than handy. The doorbell rang again before she could explain to Adam how instinctively she felt the whole project just wasn't for her. Instead she shrugged her shoulders, unthinkingly pressed the answering buzzer and promising to look at Adam's proposal properly when she had more time, opened the door to Garrett.

He stopped on the threshold, his eyes flying across the room to where Adam sat. The ready smile on his face curled into a scowl. 'I didn't realise when I rang I'd be breaking up a delicious little *ménage*,' he said sardonically, while his look covered Clarissa in dark contempt.

Clarissa gazed at him in confusion and then flushed slowly as she took in his meaning. Before she could think of an apt reply, he had crossed the room and was shaking Adam's hand with easy politeness, as if stumbling into a cosy little breakfast scene was something he did daily. Adam, Clarissa noticed, was playing it to the hilt, acting the host, offering Garrett coffee, as if he was the man of the house.

Garrett refused, explaining that the others were waiting for them in the car and that if Clarissa wasn't going to be too long, he would go down and wait with them.

At last Clarissa found her tongue, though it felt thick in her mouth. 'Adam is just going,' she explained to Garrett, and with an air of deliberate dismissal she tidied Adam's papers off the table. He rose and with impish glee pecked her lips and said goodbye.

Unable to meet Garrett's eyes, Clarissa mumbled, 'I'll be with you in a tick,' and hurried up to the bedroom to pass a brush through her hair and collect a jumper. Then, angry at herself, she slowed her movements. There was no earthly reason for her to feel flustered simply because Almighty Garrett had found her breakfasting with a friend, especially when he had simply announced that he was coming to pick her up without waiting for a yea or nay from her. She owed him no explanations.

Keeping her gestures calm, she walked slowly down the narrow staircase. She could sense Garrett's eyes raking over her and casually she slung her jumper over her shoulder before meeting his gaze.

'How you can look so damnably innocent is something I'll never fathom,' he muttered darkly. He was leaning against the kitchen counter, subtle disapproval etched in every gesture of his lithe body.

Clarissa baulked, 'It's probably because I have neither skeletons nor permanent partners stored in my closet, Mr Hamilton.' She met his eyes coolly.

Beneath his thick lashes, his pupils glittered with contained rage. Then, with a single deft movement, he was next to her, his fingers eating into her arms, pressing against the small of her back as his mouth probed hers with an urgency that set her heart pounding madly. His kiss moved through her, appropriating the rhythm of her pulse, so that when he removed his lips she felt suddenly desolate, abandoned, and she clung to him as if all separate will had left her. There was a wild look in his eyes as his mouth came down on her again and she moaned softly, as his fingers curved round her breasts, stirring them into life, sending molten waves coursing through her body.

'Did he kiss you like that?' The iciness of the voice in her ear suddenly made her draw back. His eyes bored into her and, stiffening, Clarissa pulled away from the warmth of his arms.

'Just like that!' she lashed out at him, enraged. 'Except he wasn't trying to teach me any lessons.' She threw herself on to the sofa and sat there rigidly, working to still the trembling of her legs. 'You're a sadistic brute!' she thrust at him, her voice as icy and contemptuous as his had been in her ear. 'Get out of here!'

'Only with you.' His eyes flickered over her dangerously as he pulled her to her feet. 'Let's go. We've kept the other waiting long enough.'

'The others!' she spat out at him, imagining Bianca's face if she announced to her what Garrett had been up to for the last few minutes. 'And where are you taking me, in any case?'

'To the country,' he said, his voice suddenly quiet. With a shrug he released her. 'I'm sorry—I thought after all the recent bustle and all the hard work, you might enjoy a little time off.' Her passed a lean hand through the electricity of his hair. 'I'm sorry,' he murmured again, then shaking his head with an air of wry self-mockery, 'I came up here all ready to congratulate you on a superb revision and whisk you off. You shouldn't be so damnably attractive. Or at least you might have enough modesty to keep your lovers well away from my line of vision.' The wistful smile he gave her kept any bite out of his comment and gave Clarissa no opportunity to hit back at him. She let him lead her numbly down the stairs, as she tried to make sense of her emotions.

The outside world greeted her with a blaze of sunlight, and, momentarily blinded, she leaned heavily on Garrett's arm.

'Hi!' Ted and Elinor's mingled greeting met her ears and she quickly noted that there was no sign of Bianca—no whiff of her expensive perfume. She sighed with something more than relief and relaxed into the car's upholstery. But Ted wasn't prepared after all this time of not having seen her to let her subside into silence, and willy-nilly Clarissa was drawn into spelling bees, games of geography and Twenty Questions. When they arrived at the house, Garrett uttered a stern, 'You must let Clarissa rest if she wants to.'

But Ted soon convinced her that it would be far nicer for them to have a treasure hunt out in the woods, and proceeded to monopolise her until dinner time.

Clarissa didn't mind. She felt far more herself playing games with Ted than she did either being interviewed or battling with his father. It was clear to her too that the child needed a mother, despite all Garrett's and Elinor's ministrations. The sleek Bianca didn't fulfil the role, that too was plain. At several moments during the day Clarissa was on the point of drawing Ted out on the subject, asking him if he missed his mother; but she didn't know quite how to go about it. Perhaps it would only serve to stir an area of sensitivity which was best left alone. And she had never heard Garrett mention his wife in the child's presence. Guilt, she thought. He had probably driven his wife into an early grave with that predatory Bianca of his.

But when, after having changed for dinner, she came downstairs to find Garrett seated with a rapturous Ted at the piano, Clarissa was forced to revise her earlier assessment. There was no way in which this man who was improvising complex jazz rhythms, picking threads of melody from percussive webs of sound, would intentionally hurt the little boy next to him. The bond between them seemed so strong that Clarissa suddenly felt strangely sad, a distinct outsider. Quietly she went towards the kitchen to help Elinor.

It was not until the evening meal was over, little Ted had been tucked in with a kiss, and Elinor was off watching television, that Clarissa and Garrett found themselves alone. A low fire burnt in the large living room grate. Despite the Indian summer days, evenings had begun to grow chill, and Clarissa snuggled into a large armchair close to the fire. Towering over her, his eyes glowing in the reflected light, Garrett offered her a brandy. She accepted, lazily watching his movement as he poured out the drink, the broad shoulders in the soft black sweater, the tautness of his legs beneath the black cord trousers as he eased himself into a nearby chair. Somewhere inside her a flame leapt to life and, unable to stop herself, she went to nestle on a rug by his feet.

He stroked her hair gently, 'I *am* sorry about this morning, Clarissa,' he said, his voice barely audible over the crackle of the fire.

She looked up at him, her eyes bright in the light. She had no desire to admonish him now. All she wanted was to be held in his arms—whatever his motive—to feel the texture of his skin against hers. With an audacity that amazed her, Clarissa arched her neck beneath his touch and nuzzled his arm with feathery lips. 'It doesn't matter,' she said in reply to his comment.

He surveyed her closely, ran his finger along the line

of her cheek and traced her wide curling lips. Then with an abrupt movement he rose, ostensibly to pour himself another drink. Yet when he returned, he went to sit in another chair.

'Clarissa, I want you to come to Frankfurt with me next week,' he said, his eyes focussed somewhere beyond her head. 'And don't look at me like that, or we're likely to have a repetition of this morning's little scene. There are children in the house.' His voice was suddenly stern.

Clarissa stood up as if she had been slapped. 'It doesn't strike me that you worry much about the children,' she underlined the word sarcastically, 'when Bianca is here with you. And I don't want to come to Frankfurt, thank you very much.'

A light flickered in his eyes and he looked at her from beneath half-closed lids. His arm reached out to stop her path and he drew her down on him, lifting her face to his in a long searching kiss which seemed to penetrate her entire body. 'Is this what you want, Clarissa? Is this what you've developed a taste for?' His eyes probed hers. 'Tell me.'

For a long moment she gazed into the darkness of his eyes, looked at the strong face, its wildness contained now in a brooding intelligence. And then she pulled back, gently extricating herself from his hold. How could she tell him what she wanted when she didn't herself altogether know, though she did suspect that a single kiss was not the extent of it; and that a man so plainly attached to another woman would not do.

She shrugged, and in one swift movement Garrett was on his feet. He grazed her hair with his lips. 'We'll talk about Frankfurt tomorrow, when we're both a little saner,' he said, then he was off so quickly that Clarissa could only just keep herself from running after him.

CHAPTER FIVE

CLARISSA looked out of the plane window on to thick white cloud. They would be landing in Frankfurt in about an hour and Garrett, at her side, was making notes in an appointment book. Out of the corner of her eye she watched his concentration, the set of his shoulders, and wondered at his alertness. She had woken only half an hour ago to find herself snuggled against him, his arm around her cradling her gently, and she had lurched herself into stiff wakefulness. Before they had left New York, she had made a firm resolution to herself: even though she had acquiesced to both Garrett and Elizabeth's reasoning that the trip to Frankfurt was important, that it would mean increased foreign rights sales of her new book and the others, this in no way meant that she would allow herself to succumb to Garrett and to what she now realised was an attraction so powerful that she had to be constantly vigilant to defend herself against it.

She remembered that last Sunday they had spent together in the country house. Little Ted had tumbled into her bed and announced that he was all ready to show her his favourite adventure trail. Clarissa had looked at her watch and groaned, at which point he had proceeded to tickle her into wakefulness, and they had gone down to a mountainous breakfast of pancakes and maple syrup, prepared by a smiling Garrett. It was almost, Clarissa swallowed hard, as if they were an established family; and when at lunchtime Ted had said in his inimitable way that he thought Clarissa should come and live with them, his father had looked at her with a warmth that brought a flush to her cheeks. His subsequent goodhumoured chuckle did nothing to alleviate her embarrassment.

There was a question on his face which she didn't

fully understand, and when he explained to Ted that one had to cajole a lady into such decisions, Clarissa's confusion mounted. She tried to explain to Ted as best she could that much as she liked him, she had commitments elsewhere. But the little boy only insisted that if she didn't already have a son, he couldn't understand why he couldn't be it. A twinkle in his eyes, Garrett allowed the little scene to play itself out without his intervention, and Clarissa had finished by saying that she would consider his offer seriously. At which point, Ted looked at his father triumphantly and dragged her off with him for a swim.

It was only after that that Garrett had taken her aside to his study, a room she had not previously seen and which seemed with its clear northern light, its quantities of books and contemporary prints, to be the very replica of him. Clarissa wished she had time to explore, to chat with him casually, but Garrett had instantly begun to discuss work. In a formal voice which made no allusion to any other kind of relationship between them, he had told her again how good her revision was, how he valued her co-operation both in terms of keeping to a deadline despite the odds, and with the promotional work; how he felt it was important for her to come to the Book Fair. When writers came to the Fair in person, he explained, the benefits in rights sales and sometimes even publicity were enormous. The speech finished, all Clarissa could do—unless she wanted to behave like a temperamental star, which she wasn't by nature—was agree. There had been no personal word of any kind.

Then Ted had called his father off for a moment and she had been left alone in the study. Clarissa had perused its contents, randomly picking books off the shelves and glancing through them. One of these was a book by her favourite American poet. The inscription caught her eye: 'To Laura,' it read, and Clarissa trembled slightly. His wife had tastes akin to hers. A newspaper clipping fell out of the volume and she glanced at it. A flush rose to her face, as if she had been caught in an act of voyeurism, and she quickly replaced the clipping. She didn't need a caption beneath the photograph, despite its haziness, to identify a younger Garrett and a bride with waving dark hair.

No sooner had she placed the book back on the shelf than she heard Garrett's light step on the stairs. Like a criminal, she threw herself into the nearest chair and sat there stiffly.

'Ted's begging for a game of charades before we leave,' Garrett had looked at her with a plea in his eye. 'Do you mind? I feel I have to indulge him, since I'll be away for a while.'

Clarissa exclaimed her enthusiasm, glad of anything which would take her out of this room for the time being and away from a direct confrontation with Garrett's eyes.

And now here she was minutes from Frankfurt, carrying Elizabeth's blessing and the loan of a fur coat to boot. She nibbled a roll and suddenly felt a slight irritation at the way in which she had been cajoled and manipulated into a situation she didn't altogether want: a professional union with Garrett. She turned to him coldly.

'Are my marching orders all mapped out?'

He looked at her oddly, unprepared for her tone. 'We'll play things by ear a little—though there's a fixed appointment for tomorrow with the Italians and another with the Scandinavians. As for today, you can laze about a little, catch up with jet-lag or go sightseeing, and if we're lucky I'll manage some opera tickets for this evening.'

'It hardly sounds as if you needed me here,' Clarissa mumbled ungraciously.

A devilish glint suddenly lit his eyes. 'Oh, but I *wanted* you here, little one; and director's orders must needs be obeyed.' He reached into his briefcase and brought out a transparent plastic file in which Clarissa could see the reviews of her book assembled. Waving it in her face, he said, 'And I don't know why you're grumbling. Most writers would give their eye teeth for reviews like this on a first novel, let alone the royal treatment by their publishers.'

Clarissa flushed. He was, of course, right, but she wouldn't give him that satisfaction. 'Half of those reviews don't say anything about the book. They just make a song and dance about Jethrop's—no, the almighty Garrett Hamilton's—latest discovery.'

'Ungrateful . . .' he muttered beneath his breath, and Clarissa knew from the stony face he turned on her that she had gone too far. She sat rigidly in the corner of her seat, wondering how she could just have behaved with a childish surliness so inappropriate as to be embarrassing. Garrett seemed to have the unique ability to make her behave totally out of character.

As they stepped into the chill air of the German October, Clarissa threw a half smile at the tall man at her side. He ushered her into a taxi.

'Mood improved?' He flashed a mocking look at her.

'Infinitely improved, thank you,' she said, and then with a lazy smile, added, 'I've never been to Frankfurt before. Will you tell me about the sights?'

He chuckled. 'As long as tourist guides receive better treatment than editors.'

'Editorial directors,' Clarissa bantered back. 'I love my editors.'

'We'll see what we can do about making that love extend just a little.' His eyes caressed her wickedly and then with the precision of a guide, but with a great deal more enthusiasm, he proceeded to tell her about Frankfurt, its prominence before the war, the destruction of much of the city and what was left of note.

The taxi took them to an old comfortable hotel in the centre of town, nor far from the gleaming new Opera House. It would, Garrett explained, now be full of publishers, and since they weren't particularly noted for their morals during Fair time, she had better cling to him fiercely, if she didn't want to be carried off. 'But perhaps you do?' he queried, just a hint of seriousness in his tone.

'Oh, I don't know,' Clarissa looked up at him with mock innocence. 'Given what you've advised about ways and means of improving my writing, it might all be useful material. I could give you a real bestseller next time.'

'Wretch!' He held her arm firmly, guiding her up the steps to the hotel. 'I shall have to keep my eyes on you.'

'If they're not too unhappy there,' Clarissa countered. 'I wouldn't like to deprive you of the traditional Book Fair fling.'

'Don't provoke me, Clarissa.' His eyes challenged her and he seemed to be about to say something else when the blue-eyed receptionist turned to them.

Clarissa noted the way the woman seemed to glow for Garrett, the mute little preenings and flirtatious gestures, and she was suddenly aware, as she had never quite been before, how attractive the man at her side was, with his wildly dark eyes and strong face. I must be stupid, she chided herself, blinded to the real world by my own emotional somersaults—as if I were the only woman alive, Bianca Neri apart, who could be drawn to him. The thought gave her room for pause, and with a sudden pang she hesitantly placed a hand on Garrett's arm. The receptionist looked her up and down and her manner towards Garrett changed almost imperceptibly. But Clarissa felt a tiny sense of triumph.

'And to what do I owe this little gesture of good will?' Garrett looked down at her lazily as if he had read her mind.

'The weather,' she replied playfully, but she left her hand where it was.

The room she was shown to was large and comfortable with Biedermeier solidity. Taking in her pleasure, Garrett smiled. 'You're on your own now, to rest or sightsee as you will. I'll pick you up at seven.'

She was loathe to see him go, but she nodded and managed a slightly belated thank-you.

He turned and winked at her from the door. 'I think it's the first time I've heard you say that to me. The weather is definitely improving!'

Morosely, Clarissa hung up her few garments and then, unwilling to admit the despondency she felt at being left on her own, ventured out of the hotel. She had never been to Germany before and she gazed at signs and hoardings, trying to make sense of the language. On impulse, she walked into a bank and changed some dollars into marks. Then, meandering through the streets, she came across a shop window which caught her attention.

Suits and dresses in the softest wool were temptingly displayed in a forest of autumnal colours. Thinking back on that day a little over a month ago when she had walked into Jethrop House only to be thrown into a scurry of unfamiliar activity, Clarissa made her way into the boutique. On that distant day, she had gaily dressed a character of her own creation: a pertly eccentric English miss to feed the media. Now she realised, scowling to herself and her own lack of resolve, she was half looking at herself through Garrett Hamilton's eyes. Which of the Clarissa Harlowes would he like to see? She forced this discomfiting thought away and concentrated on the clothes, finally settling on a jumpsuit in a warm russet brown, which would tuck into her high boots or could be dressed up for evening wear. Its wide matching belt fitted snugly round her waist, and she suddenly laughed as she spied herself in the mirror. Now she looked more than ever like Ted's Cheshire cat, her grin stretching from cheek to cheek, the tawny hair and eyes blending with the suit's soft wool. Her purchase completed, she romped off to buy a postcard to send to the little boy whose antics gave her so much pleasure.

Back in her room, she took a leisurely bath and lay down on the large double bed to daydream. Over the last period, while she was revising her manuscript, a new novel had begun to take shape in her, and now she nursed it along. It would, she had decided, be a book set in a city of the future, the future being the extension of some of the worst elements of the present. But her mind kept returning to the image of Garrett—the

Garrett who had stood solemnly handsome at the reception desk of the hotel; the Garrett who played the piano with his child, his eyes for once at one with his expression; the Garrett who lectured her and kissed her.

Clarissa jumped up from the bed, irritated at the vagaries of her own mind, and with a glance at her watch, angrily began to dress. She was mooning again. Could she be in love with this man? Was that why she was behaving so oddly; jealous of any woman who laid eyes on him? The thought made her drop her hairbrush and she left it lying there as she looked blindly at her wide-eyed face in the mirror. No! she groaned to herself. Sensible, intelligent, not to mention independent women didn't fall in love with arrogant unavailable men with pasts that included a wife and a child. No, she said out loud, firmly. It was only that Mr Publisher Hamilton happened to have made more of an impact on her than any man yet. Naturally enough—she explained it all away to herself—he had more power over her than any man she had yet encountered. He was older, more intelligent. He had looked into her, made her vulnerable by delving into her work. That was all. With that, Clarissa picked up her bush and passed it vigorously through her hair.

Not a minute too soon, she thought, as a knock sounded at the door and Garrett stepped in. She looked at him for a long hushed moment and then lowered her eyes. The charge of his presence suddenly made her breathless. She could feel his gaze upon her and it was almost as if he could read her thoughts, the trajectory her mind had taken over the afternoon. She shuddered, and suddenly he was close to her, lifting her chin with a gentle finger, looking into her eyes, a small smile playing round his sensuous mouth. He kissed her with feathery lips.

'More like a cat than ever tonight,' he whispered. 'I hope you don't intend to go prowling, because I have a treat in store.' He waved two tickets in the air with a jubilant grin: '*Rigoletto* at eight! And just in case you think I haven't been working for you,' he drew a diary out of his pocket, 'we have meetings lined up with every conceivable important publisher of fiction. Plus . . .' his eyes were warm with merriment, 'a surprise which I'll save for the champagne.' Suddenly he lifted her off her feet and whirled her round. 'And what a surprise!'

Infected by his mood, the laughter played in Clarissa's eyes. 'Tell me now.'

'No,' he shook his head sagely. 'Everything in good time. First I'm going to drag you downstairs for a drink and a pre-opera nibble, over which, madame author, I think it's time you told me something about yourself.' His eyes mocked her lightly, 'You do realise, Clarissa Harlowe, that although I probably know as much about your work as anyone in the world, I know nothing more about you than the four-line author biog you presented us with.'

'There isn't much to know.' Clarissa looked at him shyly, as they made their way down in the lift.

'Well, let's start from the beginning.' He led her towards a low round table in the hotel bar. 'Do you have a mother?'

'No,' Clarissa laughed. 'I sprang full-blown from my father's ear.'

'Well, that explains everything,' he smiled wryly. 'What does your father's ear do when it's not giving birth to catlike visions with enormous blue eyes?'

By the time Clarissa had munched her way through two slices of delicious pumpernickel spread with various cold meats and drunk down several glasses of white wine, so light she really had no idea she had consumed it, Garrett had learned much of what there was to know about her life.

'And now it's your turn,' she challenged him.

A dark look shadowed his face. 'My past, since it's a little longer, will take a little longer to relay,' he said with a hint of bitterness. 'So we shall have to leave it until after the opera.'

She looked at him intently. 'I do want to know.'

He shrugged and then smiled gently. 'It may be a bleak past, but it's not half as lonely as yours.'

'Lonely?' Clarissa queried. 'I wasn't lonely,' she insisted, realising that her words were only half true.

'No, you weren't lonely, you told yourself a great many stories to keep yourself company; acted so many parts, became so good at it, that until recently you even had me half convinced that you might be someone quite different.' He chuckled. 'Excellent training ground, all that, for a writer.'

'Do you think Ted is lonely, misses his mother?' Clarissa suddenly raised the subject which in one way and another she had wanted to tackle for some time.

She felt Garrett stiffen perceptibly. The dull pain in his eyes belied the optimistic note in his voice. 'I hope not. He's lively enough. There are one or two friends at school. I guess he's a bit of a loner, but that's no very bad thing.'

'Have you thought of having other children?' Clarissa brought it out with a slight tremor in her voice and wished as soon as she had spoken that she could take the words back.

His eyes seemed to bore through her. 'It's not a possibility I've wholly ruled out,' he said at last, and with an impatient gesture added, 'I think we should go.'

As they walked through the hotel lobby, Garrett was stopped twice by other publishers whom he cursorily introduced to Clarissa, and then, making apologies, whisked her off. 'We'll be bumping into people here all the time,' he explained. 'It's one of the handicaps of having been in this business for so long.'

Rigoletto, with its haunting mixture of jealousy, love and terrible revenge, brought the tears to Clarissa's eyes. When they emerged, she exclaimed, 'Now there's a hideous, heartless rake for you!'

Garrett mocked her. 'Clarissa Harlowe, full once more of tremulous nobility. You do know, dear, sweet Clarissa, that women can be equally hideous?'

'Never,' Clarissa declared adamantly.

His chuckle held a bitter note. 'Well, in my time, Clarissa . . .' He seemed to be about to tell her something and then stopped himself. Placing an arm loosely round her shoulder, he forced his voice into merriment. 'It's time to celebrate, young lady. No dour thoughts for the moment.' He whisked her back to the hotel and immediately Clarissa found herself thrust into a hubbub as acquaintance after acquaintance fell upon Garrett. Glamorous women, speaking in a variety of languages, languidly draped themselves round him, while suited men shook him by the hand. Clarissa could feel herself growing irritated as she stood on the sidelines, and when yet another fast-talking raven-haired beauty kissed him full on the lips and the smile on his face grew wider, she inched away towards the lift. There was really no place for her here and the surprise, whatever it might be, could just as well wait.

Disgruntled, she prodded the lift button and was just about to disappear when Garrett appeared at her side.

'I think you're right,' he commented blandly, taking in her air of irritation. 'We'll have dinner in my room.'

'No,' Clarissa insisted. 'I don't want to drag you away from your friends. In any case, I'm not very hungry.'

She knew she sounded like a spoiled child, but she couldn't help herself.

'Jealous, pussycat?' He arched an eyebrow at her. 'It's a good sign—makes you human like the rest of us.'

Clarissa bristled. 'Certainly not! I only thought . . .'

'Thought what?' he prodded her.

She shrugged.

'Thought you might like to be kissed as well?' His eyes mocked her as he lifted her face to his and gently grazed her lips.

Clarissa stiffened and moved away from him just as the lift door opened.

'Saved by automation,' Garrett chuckled drily, and taking her firmly by the arm led her to his room. Clarissa noted that it was right next door to hers, and while he was ringing for food, she slipped away to leave her coat and freshen up a little. The idea of having dinner in his room suddenly filled her with trepidation. It wasn't Garrett she realised she was worrying about, but herself. Could she trust herself with him, full as she was of the warring emotions which had only begun to come clear to her over the last days? But he gave her no time to reflect. Within minutes he was in her room, dragging her by the arm back to his. By the window stood a table covered with a gleaming white cloth and spread with silver. A single white rose graced a slender vase.

Garrett poured out the champagne. 'To Clarissa Harlowe,' he said melodramatically, 'who has just been nominated for the Roma Prize for the best new fiction in translation.'

Clarissa gaped at him. 'What?'

'Oh yes, Madame Harlowe. We won't know for another few days whether you've won or not, but nonetheless, the Italian critics have paid you a great honour.'

Clarissa looked at him a trifle suspiciously. 'And who are these Italian critics? Do you know them?' She was terrified that Garrett might have arranged something which in no way reflected on the nature of her work.

'Only some of them. And they have impeccable taste.' He looked at her wickedly, his eyes raking over her body, so that she could suddenly feel the way the soft wool moulded her shape. 'Now drink your bubbles and stop worrying.'

Clarissa drank down the champagne all in a gulp, letting the cool liquid tickle her throat. And then she laughed. 'Thank goodness I've finished the next book, or I'd never survive all this success!'

'You'll survive, Clarissa Harlowe.' He looked at her seriously, his eyes black beneath the jutting brow. 'Behind all that catlike softness, there beats a sturdy writer.'

Clarissa laughed again, 'I hope so.' She could feel the champagne making her head light and as he removed a silver lid to display a trayful of oysters, she passed her tongue greedily over her lips. 'Not since England!'

'And never with me.' With a lithe movement, he unfolded a gleaming white napkin on her lap, squeezed a little lemon on to a pearly shell and fed her the tang of the sea. She watched his gestures as if mesmerised, the sureness of his strong hands, the play of expressions on his mobile face, the suppleness of his body in the white shirt and dark trousers, as he moved to pour them more champagne.

A question suddenly rose to her lips, one which she had kept stifled for weeks. 'And now, Mr Publisher, tell me about yourself, about the women in your closet.'

His fork poised in mid-air, he looked at her in astonishment for a moment. She saw the expression of pain she now recognised wind across his face and then vanish as he stood up and dramatically walked towards a closet door.

'See for yourself, Miss Harlowe.' He swung the door open and a low bow entreated her to investigate. Giggling, Clarissa rose and peered into the closet.

'Empty enough for you?' Garrett breathed into her ear, and before she could answer, he had swung her round in his arms and his lips probed her mouth, at first gently and then with growing urgency. She could feel her body leap into flame as she swayed against him and a surge of pure desire thrust through her, a desire she suddenly knew had been kindling in her during all those long days since he had last held her. He looked deeply, dangerously into her eyes, his face suddenly gaunt. 'It's you I want, Clarissa, and not in my closet,' he murmured, and his lips came down on hers again with a terrible sweetness which made her press against him, so that she could feel each taut line of his body imprinted on hers. A small cry rose to her throat as his lips caressed her and his hands gently moulded her shape, finding their way to the smooth skin of her breasts, urging them to a new hardness, a shuddering sensitivity to his touch. A low moan escaped him as her own fingers sought out the satin skin of his back, the hard muscular shoulders, and her lips arched to the column of his throat.

He pulled her down on the bed beside him. 'I want you, Clarissa,' he murmured. 'God, how I want you!'

and gently, lingeringly, he trailed kisses over her eyes, her neck, the delicate mound of her bosom. Clarissa wove her hands into her hair, the bristling electricity of it against her skin playing havoc with her senses, obliterating everything but the beating of her heart in her ears and the sensation of his hands on the downy softness of her untouched skin.

Suddenly, as if a bridge were about to be crossed over which there was no returning, Clarissa drew brusquely away. Garrett looked at her, startled, his eyes molten in the half light. 'Darling, what is it?' He stroked her hair tenderly, his voice breaking from his throat.

Clarissa leapt from his touch as if it scorched her. 'Is this why you've urged me to come here, dragged me to this strange town, far away from the "children", as you call them, far away from your mistress?' she spat the words out.

She could see the storm gathering in his eyes after a momentary confusion. But he controlled it. 'No,' he uttered coldly. 'But I dare say it would have been a good enough reason. You want me, Clarissa, as much as I want you—all lessons in love aside,' he added curtly.

'Well, I'm not in the habit of sleeping with attached men,' she flung at him. 'And as for wanting, I want the moon,' she was almost in tears and she ran from the bed to stand at the window, 'the sickle moon up there!'

He was instantly at her side, his arm round her shoulders, holding her firmly. 'Attachment, as you once said to me about the self, has many guises, Clarissa,' he murmured. 'I'm sorry, I made a mistake. I did think you wanted me now, as I've wanted you for weeks. But at home, in New York, it's difficult——' His voice trailed off.

'Two-timing swine!' she turned on him, the tears now visible in her eyes.

'You might as well say three-timing, four-timing. I'm not a newborn lamb.' He gazed at her sardonically. 'I could list my commitments. There's Ted . . .'

'Oh, you don't understand anything at all,' she cut

him off, knowing the comment was childish, and with a rush, she ran back to her own room.

She flung herself down on her bed, tears pouring from her eyes. How had she ever got herself into this mess? Falling in love, yes she admitted to herself now that that was what it must be, in love with a man who belonged to someone else. Three-timing, four-timing, he had said, she suddenly remembered. Perhaps there were others. Perhaps his wife ... Clarissa remembered the woman with the dark waving hair in the hazy newspaper photograph. No, she was being gothic. He had distinctly said she was dead. Clarissa shivered: one couldn't betray the dead, she thought, be jealous of them. The living Bianca with her luminous red mouth was quite enough of a real attachment to contend with.

Yet with all that, Clarissa knew she wanted him, wanted him so desperately that if he were to come to her now, she would put aside all her qualms. No, she fumed at herself, and flung her pillow across the room, as if her traitorous self were seated there. A little dignity, Clarissa. A little less hysteria. And with a momentous effort she lay calmly on the bed forcing herself to stare glassily into the darkness until sleep overtook her.

She was woken the next morning by a soft knock at the door, followed by a black-suited man holding a tray. He placed it on the small window table, pulled back the curtains and with a *'Gut en Morgen, gnädige Fraulein,'* left her to gaze at a steely grey sky and wonder about the confusion which seemed to reel just at the brink of her consciousness.

With a start, she remembered the preceding evening and flushed hotly. How could she face Garrett today? Face all those publishers who would expect her to behave like a writer? And how did a writer behave? She shrugged and limply pulled herself out of bed to pour some steaming coffee. Its bitter flavour seemed to give her some will and she gazed at the erratic rooftops of the city doing mental accounts, just as she had done as a child before difficult moments. This and this were in her favour, this and that would be discounted. At last it seemed to her that she had worked out the balance in her own favour: there had been some successes, even though New York hype was no way to gauge anything appropriately.

Slowly she began to dress, guessing that Garrett would come to call for her very soon to take her to the Fair site. Voices from his room next door suddenly distracted her. She could hear a high-pitched woman's voice, followed by the low rumble of a male voice and then a slamming door. Suddenly Clarissa saw red. She knew in her bones that the woman must be, could only be Bianca. What was *she* doing here? Garrett had implied that now that they were away from New York ... She jabbed her foot into a pair of tights, ripping them in the process. She thrust them away from her and scrambled for another pair in her bag, angrily giving up the search and deciding on a pair of socks. She pulled on the new jumpsuit, tucked the trouser legs into boots and with a look at her scowling face in the mirror, picked up her coat and stormed into the room next door, without the least idea what she might say.

Garrett was sitting at the small bedroom desk, his broad shoulders hunched over a sheaf of papers, his face gaunt, a large hand running through his tousled hair. It suddenly occurred to Clarissa that despite the calm with which he usually met her, the time he gave her, he drove himself hard. She remembered the mention he had made of other trips in the past weeks and it dawned on her that these weren't pleasure jaunts, but work, perhaps even difficult work. The thought made her feel that she had been excessively selfish, so immersed in her own work, her own emotions, that she had somehow assumed that Garrett, as an editor, if not as a man, existed only for her.

She looked at him in momentary confusion and saw a slow smile break over his face, the two tense lines in his brow relax.

'Hello,' he said to her softly. 'Help yourself to a cup of coffee. I'll be ready in a moment.'

She noticed as she passed behind him that he seemed to be adding up a long set of figures, and she tried to make herself as unobtrusive as possible.

After a few moments he rose, knotted his tie more tightly round his neck and pulled on a soft charcoal jacket. His smile played lazily over her face. 'Sleep well?' he asked.

Clarissa swallowed hard and nodded, not trusting her voice. The deep shadows under his eyes told her he probably hadn't slept at all, and again she thought of Bianca, the voice she was sure was hers. With a forced bravery she asked, 'How many of you are there here from Jethrop House?'

He looked at her quizzically, as if the question had surprised him, then answered evenly. 'Four with Bianca, who arrived this morning. You've just missed her. She was here a few minutes ago.' The blue-black eyes suddenly twinkled. 'You two ladies are so interested in each other, I think I should get the two of you together more often.'

Clarissa felt the blood draining from her face and she stood there awkwardly.

'I'm ready when you are, Miss Harlowe.' He looked at her teasingly. 'And please don't behave as if I'm victimising you beyond repair. I'm not a totally heartless rake and you, young lady, as you've so often told me, are not the classical Clarissa, but a budding writer about to meet some prospective publishers.' With a playful gesture he lifted her chin, kissed her lightly on the lips, then seemed to be about to say something more, but changed his mind. Instead he looked into her eyes, deeply, seriously, for a moment, before suggesting that they really should be off.

Clarissa didn't know quite what she had been expecting the Frankfurt Bookfair to be like but it certainly wasn't what finally confronted her. Somehow books had conjured up the idea of libraries, stately old halls, muted conversation. But instead she found a vast modern exhibition site, teeming with people. Several sprawling buildings assembled in a row housed

publishers and this year's collections. Each had a
number and were serviced by a special bus, far too
small for the crowds of participants who mobbed the
fair. Garrett explained that only two of these buildings
were central to them: one held the American and
European publishers, Germans apart, who had their own
building and one which was far more packed than the
others, since the citizens of Frankfurt, not to mention
publishers, booksellers and media people from everywhere in Germany, poured into this hall to view up-
and-coming books.

The building Garrett and Clarissa finally entered was
more akin to an airport than anything she had
imagined: with its artificial atmosphere, food kiosks,
wine bars, steady hum of voices speaking many
tongues, and rows upon rows of book displays, one stall
more lavish than the next. As Garrett led her down
these numbered rows towards the Jethrop House stand,
she was overwhelmed by the sheer quantity and
diversity of books, made dizzy by the sheer number of
people, all of whom seemed to have something to do
with the making and marketing of what she had always
considered to be somewhat unique products. She felt
herself growing smaller and more insignificant by the
second, like Alice dropping through her looking glass.
Garrett took one look at her face and squeezed her
hand.

'Horrendous, isn't it? But don't worry, it will all soon
grow familiar.'

Clarissa shook her head in dismay, 'I don't think I'll
ever write again. There are simply too many of us!'

'Hush,' he gave her a stern look. 'All this is to do
with me. The business of disseminating your work.
And it is a business, Clarissa. There's little point in
burying your head in the ground and thinking
otherwise. That's what I was trying to make clear to
you in New York.'

She scowled. Jethrop House was bad enough. But
this fair ... turning every private thought, every book,
into a marketable commodity! She was about to

LOVE BEYOND REASON
There was a surprise in store for Amy!

Amy had thought nothing could be as perfect as the days she had shared with Vic Hoyt in New York City—before he took off for his Peace Corps assignment in Kenya.

Impulsively, Amy decided to follow. She was shocked to find Vic established in his new life. . . and interested in a new girl friend.

Amy faced a choice: be smart and go home. . . or stay and fight for the only man she would ever love.

MAN OF POWER
Sara took her role seriously

Although Sara had already planned her escape from the subservient position in which her father's death had placed her, Morgan Haldane's timely appearance had definitely made it easier

All Morgan had asked in return was that she pose as his fiancée. He'd confessed to needing protection from his partner's wife, Louise, and that part of Sara's job proved easy

But unfortunately for Sara's heart, Morgan hadn't told her about Monique. . .

Your Romantic Adventure Starts Here.

THE LEO MAN
"He's every bit as sexy as his father!"

Her grandmother thought that description would appeal to Rowan, but Rowan was determined to avoid any friendship with the arrogant James Fraser.

Aboard his luxury yacht, that wasn't easy. When they were all shipwrecked on a tropical island, it proved impossible.

And besides, if it weren't for James, none of them would be alive. Rowan was confused. Was it merely gratitude that she now felt for this strong and rugged man?

THE WINDS OF WINTER
She'd had so much—now she had nothing

Anne didn't dwell on it, but the pain was still with her—the double-edged pain of grief and rejection.

It had greatly altered her; Anne barely resembled the girl who four years earlier had left her husband, David. He probably wouldn't even recognize her—especially with another name.

Anne made up her mind. She just had to go to his house to discover if what she suspected was true. . .

EXTRA BONUS
MAIL YOUR ORDER TODAY AND GET A FREE TOTE BAG FROM HARLEQUIN.

Canada Post
Postes Canada
708

expostulate on the fact, when they were stopped by a dark, vibrant man with flashing eyes.

'Garrett Hamilton!' He embraced him and kissed him on both cheeks. 'What a pleasure to see you!' which was all Clarissa grasped in the ensuing flow of Italian, until Garrett introduced her and Signor Fiorucci proceeded to shake her hand with unmistakeable warmth.

'The brilliant young Signorina Harlowe. I am so very pleased to make your acquaintance. Shall we sit down and have a cup of coffee?'

Garrett apologised for them, saying he had to check in at his stand, but they would meet later in the day, perhaps for dinner that evening as well. *'Benissimo!'* Signor Fiorucci exclaimed, 'It will be a pleasure to have a chance to speak to you and the Signorina.'

'That,' Garrett explained, 'was your Italian publisher.'

'Oh!' Clarissa flushed, feeling decidedly stupid.

But from that moment on she had little opportunity to reflect on any of her own feelings. At the Jethrop House stand, she was handed an appointment book, already filled with meetings, and when Garrett wasn't ushering her off to one appointment or another, to set after set of drinks or coffee, the Jethrop House foreign rights person was. Clarissa's head reeled with names and interrupted conversations and she didn't quite know whether she was making a complete fool of herself or sounding decidedly witty. When at four o'clock she found herself alone for a moment, she breathed a sigh of relief and was happy to idle anonymously down the British aisles of the building, gaze randomly at a few titles which caught her attention.

'Clary—well, I never!' The sound of her childhood name made her spin round in disbelief.

'Michael!' She threw herself into a pair of strong arms and found herself lifted well off her feet.

'You didn't tell me you were going to be here,' they both exclaimed in unison, and then with a burst of laughter Clarissa stared happily into her brother's beloved face.

'Let me look at you.' He held her at arm's length and Clarissa gazed at what she knew was a male replica of herself: the same bristling chestnut hair, wide blue eyes, straight nose and curling mouth, but all put together in a male mould and a larger frame.

'Just the same,' he squeezed her, 'but more beautiful than ever—and more successful, from what I hear. Your name's been making the rounds, and I feel quite honoured to be your brother.'

'And you must have been promoted too, if you're here,' Clarissa teased him. 'You never said.'

He chuckled. 'You know those letters of ours never seem to deal with anything as tangible as that! But come on, Clary, let me buy you a bottle of celebratory champers and we can catch up on real things.'

With a feeling of pure delight, Clarissa let her brother lead her to the nearest wine bar and there she sat, snuggled next to him, forgetting everything but the delight of being with him again.

When they had caught up on the most pressing round of details, Michael casually asked her, 'And how many New York beaux have you got under your hat?'

She stared at him, the familiar face posing the familiar yearly question, to which she always answered in comic ritual, 'But, Michael, you know you've spoiled me to the possibility of any other man.'

He saw her pause and a slow grin broke over his face. 'Unbelievable! I do think someone at long last has managed to dent Clary's imaginative armour. I don't know whether I should bow down and pay my respects to this heroic Siegfried or be madly jealous.'

Clarissa put her hand on his arm and looked sternly into his eyes. 'It's nothing, Michael. Just a . . .'

'Well, attachments do indeed come in many guises!' An icy voice behind her made her twist round in alarm. Garrett Hamilton loomed behind her, Bianca Neri, her flowing blonde hair glinting against a sleek black dress, at his side. 'You realise that you've altogether missed your appointment with the Swedish publisher,' he glared at her, 'and I've been busily making apologies for you, claiming you must be lost somewhere in these vast halls.'

Clarissa flushed, as much in anger at his lack of politeness as out of embarrassment at having forgotten the appointment.

'I'll be off now, Clary. I can see you're busy.' Michael gave her a long slow wink. 'I'll give you a ring at your hotel later and we can arrange to get together.' And before she had had a chance to introduce him to Garrett, he was off.

'You know that we've brought you here to work.' Garrett lowered his long body into Michael's chair and eyed her dangerously.

'I told you there wasn't much point,' said Bianca in a voice so low that her words were barely audible.

Clarissa was suddenly enraged. What right did he have to talk to her in that tone, embarrass her in front of her brother and the loathsome Bianca who seemed to be looking at her as if she were some piteous insect?

'Work,' she snapped at him. 'My work is at my desk.—This,' she gestured at the vast hall, 'this is just more of your bloody publisher's exploitation. More pennies for the Jethrop House account. Talk to your marketing director about it,' she lashed out at Bianca. 'you have a lot more in common with her than you'll ever have with me!'

'Your prejudices are becoming something of a strain, Clarissa,' she heard him say behind her. But she had already rushed off, the tears brimming at her eyelids, and she suddenly found herself outside, coatless, an icy wind chilling her to the bone. Yet she wouldn't give him the satisfaction of crawling back in there to get her coat. There would be a taxi soon enough if she managed to get to the front gates of the Fair. And all the wine she had swallowed today would protect her.

She reached her hotel room, only to feel once again like a complete fool. And an utterly miserable one. If she had nurtured any secret hopes that Garrett would somehow magically prefer her over Bianca, want her for more than a holiday fling, she had now most certainly alienated him for good. So be it, she resolved, as she tried tearfully to ride the tide of an ache so pervasive that it seemed to take over the core of her being.

CHAPTER SIX

An hour later a cold, distant voice spoke to Clarissa over the telephone. 'We're waiting for you downstairs, I've got your coat.'

She shuddered and worked to compose her features into a semblance of normality. With a horrified glance at her reflection, she changed into her suede suit, pulled a pair of warm brown tights over her slender legs and on top of these, some striped leg-warmers. The German October seemed far colder to her than any English winter she could remember.

She knew as she made her way to the lobby that she owed Garrett some kind of apology for her outburst, but she couldn't convince herself that she was altogether in the wrong; nor could she think how to go about it. She saw Garrett at once, seated in the midst of a small group which included the Italian publisher. His face was animated in conversation, his eyes droll with the humour of his speech. Clarissa hesitated as she felt her heart take on a mad rhythm, which she attributed to fear as much as anything else.

He saw her and a dark look crossed his face, to be replaced immediately by a wide, encouraging smile, as he rose to greet her. Clarissa shivered as his lips touched her cheek. 'Best behaviour, Scout's honour,' he whispered, and then casually draping his arm round her shoulder, he led her towards the group.

As if I were some temperamental child who needed to be cajoled! she thought to herself, admitting wryly that in part that was how she had behaved.

She did her best to make amends, even stiffly saying to Bianca, 'I'm sorry about my outburst earlier. The Fair is exhausting.' And then she turned to Signor Fiorucci, eagerly answering his questions, easily falling into a conversation which ranged over the length and

breadth of English literature. His flashing eyes seemed
to embrace her warmly. 'I hope you shall come and stay
with me in Rome if you win the prize,' he said to her.
'My son Marco, who works in our publishing house,
would be delighted to meet you.'

Clarissa thanked him, saying that would indeed be
wonderful, but she doubted whether she was good
enough for such honours.

They were joined by a grave, elderly man who turned
out to be the Swedish publisher whom she had failed to
see that afternoon. Clarissa gave Garrett a grateful look
as he introduced her and again apologised for having
missed the appointment. 'I haven't learned to be
businesslike enough yet,' she said to the elderly man.
'And out of the most wonderful coincidence, I bumped
into my brother whom I haven't seen for months and
we just lost ourselves in talk. So, no appointment.' She
shrugged. 'I *am* sorry.'

'That's all right, my dear,' the elderly man replied.
'I'm very happy to have the opportunity to meet you
now.'

Clarissa could feel Garrett's eyes blazing into her.
'Youre brother?' he queried, looking at her intently.

'Yes. I wanted to introduce you, but I think you
scared him away.'

A wide smile played over his features. 'I didn't know
I was quite so frightening.'

'Rather!' she exclaimed.

'Let's keep it that way,' he chuckled wickedly, and
then with easy grace, he rose to his feet and shepherded
them all towards a taxi which ferried them across a
bridge to Frankfurt's old town and a small homey
restaurant reputed for its seafood. 'And publishing
sharks,' Garrett quipped.

Clarissa thought she had never seen him in such good
form, his eyes as sparkling as his conversation, his face
dramatically handsome as he engaged the company
with his ready wit. He seemed, she noted as he talked to
the many acquaintances who joined their table at
regular intervals, to stand head and shoulders above

anyone at his side. When his eyes met hers to draw her into the group, she looked away from him, afraid he would read the warmth she knew must be written there.

She eyed Bianca surreptitiously, trying hard not to let her irritation at the woman's possessiveness show, and she even tried to chat to her about this and that. At one moment she heard Signor Fiorucci, who sat diagonally opposite her, ask Garrett, 'And how are you managing without Laura?' Clarissa's ears perked up at this reference to Garrett's wife. But she missed his response, as Bianca questioned her, for once without a note of hostility in her voice.

'I'm impressed at the way you managed to finish your revision, despite the stolen manuscript. But perhaps you'd rather you hadn't, given how little you're enjoying the Fair.'

'I do feel like a fish out of water,' Clarissa admitted.

Bianca weighed her remark and then smiled, almost kindly. 'I guess it is a ghastly place—though I always enjoy it. I did try to tell Garrett that it would be mad to bring you here.' Without waiting for Clarissa to respond, she turned to Garrett. 'You see, Clarissa agrees that she would have been happier not to come to the Fair.'

Signor Fiorucci laughed, 'But then I wouldn't have had the pleasure of meeting you.'

Clarissa flushed, not knowing quite how to extricate herself. She noticed that Garrett was looking at her quizzically. But before she could say anything, he returned to his conversation with Fiorucci and the Swede, and Bianca enthusiastically joined in. They were discussing a new popular science series and how it could be sold to schools. Feeling more and more of an outsider, Clarissa watched them. Garrett didn't seem to mind either Bianca's comments or the way she pawed him. Her heart sank, and when the company went back to the hotel to congregate once more at the bar, she bade them all goodnight. She didn't want to have to be masochistically present at a scene where Garrett went off with Bianca and she was left dismally stranded.

In her room, Clarissa tried to focus on other things. She was grateful for the telephone message from her brother asking whether he could meet her for dinner the following evening. At least Michael would provide an edge of sanity, relate her to a self she was no longer altogether sure she inhabited. With that comforting thought and with a sense of fatigue compounded by too many glasses of wine, Clarissa just managed to keep her last waking thoughts from tumbling into a depression of which the greatest part was longing.

The following day seemed to be a heightened version of the first, and she began to understand why the Fair was called such. The spirit which prevailed seemed to be that of a carnival—perhaps a carnival at which the marketing instinct was supreme—but a carnival nonetheless. Although her appointments with publishers seemed to be over, Clarissa found herself tossed into a television show in the German part of the Fair—a show which was relayed both there and in the U.S. and contained some writers whose names she held in awe. She spent most of her time listening to them intently and not daring to utter more than an occasional word before these honoured beings.

Her meeting with her brother was sheer delight, but for the first time in her life she couldn't quite bring herself to tell him about a part of herself, though he pressed her with schoolboy zeal and devilishly added, 'Your publisher, that Hamilton character, seems to have an excellent reputation, despite the horrid picture you drew of him in your letters. I thought he'd have dollar signs for eyes.' When she flushed, he added, 'Though he did treat you a little brusquely yesterday.'

Clarissa looked at her brother strangely, wanting to confide in him, but somehow not being able to. In the past there hadn't been anything they couldn't share, and this intrusion of a new reality made her somehow sad, added a dimension of potential loneliness.

Michael noted her mournful air and chided her, 'Come on, Clary. You've got to grow up some time, you know.'

When he asked her whether she had any plans about coming back to England, Clarissa shrugged. She realised that here was another first: her life no longer seemed simple, self-determined by her desire to write. She seemed to be waiting, unclear about her next steps. She lashed herself with self-contempt. What she should really be concentrating on was her next book, not this strange creature of a man who left her emotions in a raw jumble.

On the second to last day of the Fair, she happened to be sitting at the Jethrop stand, her own book on display behind her, with only Bianca Neri for company. It was the first time she had been alone with the woman, and Clarissa tried to find something to say to the tall languid blonde who kept crossing and uncrossing her long silken legs as if they were reptilian appendages.

'Do you think my coming here has been worthwhile, has helped the book?' Clarissa tried to find the only subject they might have in common.

Bianca looked at her with something which seemed to be akin to real interest. 'Yes, it probably has, I have to admit,' she said. And then with a tone of complicity, she added, 'Garrett's been working you to the bone, hasn't he? He's behaving like a madman. You know, of course, he's doing it all on a dare?'

Clarissa gazed at her with a blank expression. 'A dare?' she queried.

'Yes, a dare,' Bianca laughed. 'I was there the day it all happened. You don't really think Garrett is *seriously* interested in your work?' She looked at Clarissa, openly assessing her slightness, her youth.

Clarissa's pulse began to beat in apprehension. 'What happened? What dare?' she asked, forcing her voice to be even.

The woman smiled and conjured up the scene as if she had been relishing its moments simply for Clarissa's hearing. 'It was at a board meeting, about six or eight weeks before your book was to be published. The directors came down hard on Garrett and told him he'd have to cut the new fiction list by half. The sales simply weren't shaping up. He was furious! He railed at them, told them in so many words that if the accountants allowed as much time and money for marketing serious new fiction as they did for other parts of the list, it could be made to work.

'I remember,' Bianca chuckled, 'old Hargreaves stood up and said, "Very well, Garrett, if that's a dare, I challenge you to flick through the autumn list at random, pick a title and promote it to your heart's delight. If you can make it work and pay, fine and well. If not, we cut." Garrett was amazingly cool. He picked up the catalogue, and as if he were playing one of those bible divination games, he opened it at random and pointed a finger. Your book turned up on the lottery. I doubt whether he'd even read it before that moment.' Bianca took in the light of dawning recognition on Clarissa's face with a look of unalloyed pity.

'I see,' Clarissa said quietly.

'And when Garrett takes something on, he takes it on with a vengeance. I know him well,' Bianca added, crossing her legs again. 'We've been together for a long time now. It's almost like being married . . . even to the point where he occasionally has flings with other women.' She looked at Clarissa to make sure her meaning had been clear. 'Yes, I know Garrett almost too well,' she sighed, and took a long puff of her cigarette. 'And that's why he pushed you so hard on the manuscript too, worked on it like a lunatic himself—all those pages of notes he provided you with on how to put a little sexual tension into the text.' She met Clarissa's eyes with a gaze of utter incomprehension. 'Though you'd think a woman would know all that in her bones.'

Clarissa felt herself growing deathly pale. Just how much had Garrett recounted to Bianca? Had he also given her graphic details of his lessons in love as they laughed over her together, probably in bed? She gripped the arms of her chair so tightly that her fingers seemed to become part of the metal.

Bianca continued, her eyes sparkling at the impact her words were having. 'Well, all that rush so that he could get the foreign rights people geared up, and my staff, the sales people.' She chuckled, 'Yes, Garrett will use you to the last iota of your strength, charm you until you think he's Jupiter incarnate, in order to get his way with his books. Quite ruthless.' She smiled widely as if it was a quality which met with all her approval. 'But you mustn't take any of it personally. I remember,' a gleam came into her eyes, 'when we were talking things over after the initial board meeting, he looked at your photograph and groaned, "At least she's not too hideous."'

The woman uncrossed her long legs, flashed Clarissa a brittle smile and looked at her watch. 'Well, it's time for my next appointment. See you, Clarissa. Don't be too upset. It's the way of publishers and you'll do well out of it.'

Clarissa sat staring blankly into space, oblivious of the noise and bustle around her. She suddenly knew what those cartoon characters must feel like after they had been flattened by steamrollers or pounded into non-existence by weighty hammers. She was aware that she had put the next hour aside to have a long chat with her English publisher, that slightly absentminded old gentleman who had always treated her like a rather precious granddaughter, and she walked off to see him now, wondering that her feet could still carry her, that her tongue seemed to make articulate sounds and that her face seemed to contort itself into expressions which others recognised as intelligible.

Then she wandered back to the hotel, walking the distance through the gloomy end-of-day Frankfurt streets. As she approached the train station in which the Turkish and Yugoslav migrant labourers congregated their tired, drawn faces a testimony to the way in which their host country treated them, she thought for a moment that she might simply board a train and find her way back to London, away from all this, away from Garrett. But the energy this kind of decision required was beyond her and by a slow random route, she eventually made her way to the hotel, changed into her nightie and lay on her bed to stare uncomprehendingly at the ceiling.

The more she thought about it, the more she realised that Bianca's story should give her no cause for surprise. It revealed, except in its brazen details, no more than she had already accused Garrett of on a number of occasions. His priority was to sell books, no matter what they contained. Yet, whatever her outbursts at him indicated, she had grown to believe that he did care, and not only about her work. To choose her name at random from a list was almost forgivable. But how could he laugh with Bianca about her book, about his lessons in love? Clarissa shuddered, forcing herself to try to see it all not as a shocking revelation, but simply as an extended explanation of already observable facts. It was only a question of learning how to keep her stupid, bleeding heart out of it. She couldn't allow herself to love a man who was— as Bianca had underlined—as good as married.

'Clarissa!' an exuberant voice called her out of her daze, closely followed by the presence she least wanted to be confronted with. He had come in through the adjoining door which she had forgotten to lock, and he paused as he saw her stretched out on the bed.

'Clarissa, what is it?' He was instantly at her side, and she read in his face that she must present a shocking sight. He sat down at the edge of the bed and his taut fingers caressed her face as he looked at her anxiously. 'What is it, Clarissa? Have you had bad news from home?'

She shook her head, steeling herself against the sensation his touch stirred in her. 'Just tired,' she said as evenly as she could.

'My poor, pale darling,' he murmured, stroking her skin with light lips. Clarissa kept herself rigid against him, even when his lips delicately fondled hers. His eyes posed a question, but she looked obliquely away from him, edging along the bed so that his dangerous proximity would not totally engulf her. He shrugged, looking suddenly tired. 'I thought you'd want to know,' he said, his voice noncommittal, 'that you've won the prize. Fiorucci leaked it to me this afternoon. He wants you to come to Rome to receive it next week. I got carried away,' his lips curled wryly. 'I thought you might enjoy a little holiday after all this and I booked a flight to Rome for tomorrow morning. I arranged for Ted and Elinor to join us the day after,' he added simply, then stood up, looking down on her from what seemed a very great height.

Clarissa's first impulse was to throw her arms around him, and the effort of willing herself not to do so made her movements stiffly artificial. 'That's very kind,' she said. 'It's good news.'

'You don't sound very enthusiastic.' He eyed her sceptically.

She shrugged. 'It will help to promote the books, help sales.' Her own strained voice sounded strange to her.

'Yes, promotion. That's what all this is about, isn't it?' Garrett said bitterly.

'That's what you wanted,' she said, feeling she would choke if he didn't leave the room soon.

'And you didn't?' His eyes accused her. 'You're going to tell me you're not pleased that your two novels are going to be translated into several European languages?'

'Yes, I'm pleased,' she said, her voice bitter with the thought that she would have willingly given up all the translations just to be able to hold him without the spectre of Bianca hanging over her. 'But right now, all I want to do is sleep.'

'Sleep, then,' he said, his voice rough. He looked at her intently for a moment, his eyes glancing savagely over her supine shape. Then he turned on his heel, and though he closed the door lightly, she felt its reverberations as if he had slammed it thunderously behind him.

When she woke from a troubled sleep the next morning,

Clarissa felt she would explode. The shock of Bianca's story had turned into seething anger. So he thinks I'm not *too* hideous; so they laugh together about my sexual naïveté, she told her image in the mirror. Right, I'll show him! And there were other, more troubling things she wanted to show him too. If he could use her, ride blatantly over her private core so as almost to obliterate its separate existence for his own purposes, then she had no intention of being a mere passive victim; one of the used in the great well-oiled system, even if it seemed from the outside that she too had benefited from Garrett's promotional work. No, she could use him too, though what that meant in terms of concrete action, Clarissa wasn't too sure. All she knew was that here she was with a man who had consciously woken her into feeling simply to make her pliable to his wishes, his business interests, to fulfill a passing sexual urge, as well. There hadn't been any need for it, she stormed to herself. She would have been quite co-operative enough without all that. And not only had he woken her into feeling, into love—she derided herself—but had done it with the full knowledge that he was attached. And now she could concentrate on nothing but him. There were no words in the moral hierarchy bad enough for a man like that.

Dressing herself as best she could in her anger, Clarissa grew irritated with her image and flounced into Garrett's room as casually as he had into hers.

He was stretched out on the bed, his chest bare, reading a morning paper and he looked up at her in surprise.

She didn't quite know what she had expected to find, perhaps Bianca with him, perhaps she had wanted a scene, but the image of him lying there, his muscled shoulders rippling against the sheets, his eyes smiling at her lazily, disconcerted her, stopped her in her tracks.

'Feeling better?' he asked.

'Much,' she said in a staunch voice, and attempting casualness, she went to sit by his side. She knew from the thudding of her pulse that whatever she was going to do was not going to be easy; that whatever vague plans she had of using him as he had used her might backfire to her own disadvantage, but with a devil-may-care recklessness she plunged ahead. She trailed her hand lightly over the smoothness of his chest, fingering the rugged tufts of dark curly hair, trying desperately to keep her mind free of the sensations the touch aroused in her, wanting only to hurt him so that he could feel how he had hurt her, and by the same tactics.

He looked at her strangely and stopped her hand. With a little pout, she lowered her face close to his.

'Changed your mind, Clarissa?' he asked softly.

She didn't answer him, but instead she moved her lips along his shoulder, willing herself to keep cool as his arms rose to embrace her and draw her closer to him. There was a laughing glint in his eyes as his lips met hers, and for a moment, the force of his kiss, the sheer male scent of his skin, overpowered her so totally that she felt she might drown in him. Then, keeping the image of Bianca and Garrett laughing about her in the forefront of her mind, she pressed herself sensuously against him, triumphing in the sense of his growing passion, the tautness of his body against hers. He kissed her again, probing her mouth with a burning ferocity, and at that moment she pulled away abruptly and got to her feet.

'See you some time, Mr Publisher,' she thrust at him, her voice savage. 'Thanks for all the good things you've done for my brilliant career. And for my sexual awakening!' With that she slammed his door behind her and went back into her own room. Her heart pounding, she gathered up her few things and flung them in her bag. But she was only half way to the door before he stormed behind her, grasping her shoulders and forcing her to turn towards him.

'What the hell do you think you're up to?' rage contorted his face and she could see the pulse throbbing at his neck.

'Oh, a little lesson in love,' she looked at him with all the coolness she could muster. 'I thought it was time you saw it from the other side.'

His face seemed to turn to stone. Only his eyes burned with untempered rage, and Clarissa was suddenly afraid he might hit her. Instead he said in an icy voice, 'You should finish what you've begun.' He gripped her with iron fingers and his mouth bit into her, forcing her, willing her to respond. Only when she felt her breath was no longer her own did he relax his hold, and the sweet urgency of his kiss, the play of his hands on her back, the delicate skin of her neck, made her cling to him of her own accord. Then coolly he distanced himself, only loosely trailing his fingers on her shoulders. 'I don't know what's brought all this on, Clarissa. But don't play games with me. And don't start what you're unwilling to finish.' His dark eyes threatened her. Then, as if he were suddenly tired, he turned away. 'I'll be ready in ten minutes. We can have breakfast downstairs and then go. You can make your mind up at the airport as to which plane you're taking.'

Clarissa slumped into a chair and watched his receding shape. She felt devoid of all energy. He was right. She shouldn't play games at which she was a child and he an expert. But then she could do nothing but resign herself to the fact that she was madly, stupidly in love with a man who—despite all his seeming kindness—used her, who recounted their moments together to another woman; a man who was not destined for her. She sat there bleakly, rising only when he poked his head through the door to see whether she was ready, and then with an effort at dignity, following him.

'You know Fiorucci assumes you'll be in Rome for the prize-giving,' he said to her seriously over the breakfast table.

'And you wouldn't want me to disappoint my Italian publisher, is that right?'

'Nor Ted,' he added.

Clarissa flushed. 'That's blackmail!'

'At the moment I'm willing to adopt any tactics.'

Her mouth dropped, but he cut off her response. 'You don't give me much choice, Clarissa, do you?' A smile played round his lips. 'Besides, you'll enjoy it. Rome's quite a nice place.'

On the flight, Garrett was at his most charming, and after one swingeing aside in which she asked him how he had managed to dump Bianca so easily—to which he responded only by looking at her curiously—Clarissa reminded herself that she was going to be dignified, going to act responsibly rather than emotionally. And she succeeded in behaving with an interested politeness which was almost natural. He told her how he had a particular soft spot for Rome: home town to his stepmother and stepsister before his father had brought them to America. They now lived in Florence and perhaps he would visit them.

Clarissa's ears perked up. She had never heard anything more about his family than that his father was something of a madcap building constructor who had a magpie instinct for the *bric-à-brac* of European civilisation. Garrett smiled when she reminded him that he had mentioned this to her.

'Yes, I think the additions to the family were made in something of the same spirit,' he commented drily.

'And your mother?' Clarissa asked, genuinely curious.

'She died when I was twelve,' he informed her. 'I still remember her vividly. Father remarried very soon after. He didn't know how to live without a woman.'

Just like you, Clarissa was about to say as she thought of his wife and then Bianca and the countless other women Bianca's comments had conjured up. But she kept her thoughts to herself and Garrett hastily changed the subject, as if any talk which might lead to his personal life was a gross infringement. And this, she thought unkindly to herself, is the man who wanted me to bare my soul for the television cameras! She couldn't hold back on that score.

'For someone who believes in the promotion of the self,' she said to him as they were disembarking, 'you are assiduously secretive.'

'Ah, but you forget,' he looked at her astutely, 'I

don't write books either. None of my experience is for public consumption.'

The comment angered her, especially in the light of what he must have told Bianca about them. 'My books aren't about my life,' she insisted emphatically.

His eyebrows shot up in mock astonishment, and then he seemed to censor what he was about to say, commenting instead, 'No, not yet, that's true. They're still only about the child in you.'

Clarissa pondered that remark as they drove from the airport into Rome. Garrett had hired a car, a large comfortable Lancia which hugged the motorway snugly and which he drove with Italian expertise, nipping in and out of traffic at heart-stopping pace. But when the graceful hills of the eternal city came into sight, she forgot everything except what was in front of her. Garrett took in her rapt face and chuckled, 'You see, Clarissa, even our road leads to Rome. You are pleased you decided to come, aren't you?'

She could only smile at him in return as the city slowly unfolded before her, the remarkable avenues graced by the imperial monuments of an ancient people, the curling Tiber reflecting the warm ochre of stately buildings in oblique autumnal light, the many fountains around which dark-eyed children frolicked.

They pulled up in front of an elegant hotel, surrounded by patrician gardens and close to the Villa Borghese. Clarissa glowed.

'As soon as I've dropped my bags, I want to walk, to walk for hours.'

'In company or alone?' Garrett's eyes teased her.

'As you like,' she replied stiffly.

'I don't know,' he mused for a moment. 'It might just do you good to have your rump pinched by a few eager Romans.'

Her cheeks coloured in confusion.

As it was, they walked together, and Clarissa was grateful. She couldn't have asked for a better, more amenable companion, and the one time she strayed from him in a crowded flea market and found herself assiduously followed and chatted up, she was all the more thankful to see Garrett's handsome face towering over others and beckoning to her from a short distance.

'I warned you,' he smiled warmly, but when he moved to take her arm she froze, rigid at his touch and ungraciously pulled her arm away. He shrugged, and made nothing of the incident, taking her off instead to eat a *pizza calzone*—a pizza in pants, he explained, all its cheesy essence protected by its doughy clothing. By the time they had wandered back to the hotel, Clarissa thought even her walk-loving feet would drop.

Garrett's spirits, on the other hand, seemed unflagging.

'What shall it be this evening, Signorina Harlowe, culture or pleasure?' his blue-black eyes twinkled at her.

'Doesn't the first necessarily include the second?' she said to him sententiously, suddenly frightened.

He laughed outright. 'Necessarily,' he said. 'I was only worried about the state of your wakefulness.'

Clarissa relaxed, 'Well, then I think we could settle for the culture of food and,' she added, a little embarrassed, as if she were conveying an enormous secret. 'I'd like to sit in one of those terrazzi on the Via Veneto and watch all the grand people on parade. And the papparazzi. Do they really exist?'

'In Technicolor splendour,' Garrett assured her, and urged her to put on her most extravagant outfit.

Clarissa's face fell. 'My most extravagant outfit was hired from a shop in New York and returned as soon as it had confronted that dreadful Gordon Foster.'

'Well, we shall have to see to that Signorina Harlowe. I can't be seen in front of the papparazzi, let alone Roman prize-winners with a mini-skirted scamp. Can you manage a few more steps?'

Clarissa nodded, too tired to take offence at his words and knowing within herself that he was simply teasing her goodnaturedly. She sighed inwardly. How she wished she could allow herself to love this man openly, freely.

The few more steps brought them to a small boutique

which displayed only a few garments, but these tailored to such perfection that Clarissa gasped with craftsman's delight at what she recognised as expert workmanship. 'I couldn't,' she said shyly to Garrett.

'Unless you want to walk any further, that's all there is.'

'But the prices!' she exclaimed.

He shrugged his shoulders impatiently. 'My present.'

Clarissa protested, but he wouldn't budge and finally added, 'All right, Ted's and my present.'

'That's blackmail,' she laughed.

'Only if you believe in bartering systems. I'd prefer to see it as a gratuitous act.'

Finally she acquiesced. She was more than half excited at the thought of trying on clothes she would otherwise never have dared to approach—like dressing a heroine again, she thought to herself.

In fact it was Garrett and the boutique owner who dressed her. With an expert's glance, the small elegant man looked her over. Then with busy gestures, he pulled out three garments and matching accessories: a swirling misty rose skirt with a blouse of sheerest organza, its pleated front and flowing sleeves a delight to the eye and the hand; a black high-necked dress whose tiny folds moulded the body in stillness and swung into a full circle when Clarissa moved; and a metallic blue suit, simply tailored. Garrett insisted that she have the first two garments, and forgetting herself, she kissed him exuberantly on the lips, promising that she would buy him something equally extravagant on the morrow.

Thrilled with her new clothes, she showered and changed excitedly, and forgot everything in the exhilaration of a night amidst the marvels of Rome, the exquisite food, elegantly served, the animated people parading as if for the movie cameras, their eyes meeting flirtatiously, speaking volumes in a language of lashes and pupils, as if all this were the norm of everyday encounters. She laughed out loud as she compared it mentally with a London tube, where all eyes bore intransigently down on newspapers and away from human contact.

She explained her laughter to Garrett, meeting his eyes in imitation of Italian gestures. The force of the contact made her tremblingly aware of the potent attraction of the man in front of her, and she stopped her narrative in mid-sentence, colouring in emotion.

He mistook her sudden silence. 'Tired, Clarissa? Shall we call it a day?'

She nodded, needing now to get away from him if she were not to betray the fullness of her feelings. To compose herself, she conjured up what Bianca had told her, made herself recall that having used her for his own purposes, Garrett was now simply being ordinarily friendly. The Roman prize was as important to him as to her, and he needed her to behave well, receive it publicly. His charm was merely a tool—one he could turn on anyone when it suited his needs. That was something she must not let herself forget, whatever his surface graciousness.

She accompanied him stiffly back to the hotel, and when having opened the door of her room for her, he turned to kiss her, she pulled brusquely away. 'Don't touch me,' she said stiffly. 'Go back to your Bianca. Leave me alone!'

The surprise in his rugged face turned to anger, but the storm gathering in his eyes led only to a single gesture. 'If that's how you feel, Clarissa. If that's how you feel,' he shrugged, and closed the door firmly behind him.

The next day when she rose, Clarissa learned from reception that he had gone out. Good riddance, she thought. The two-timing bastard, with his mistresses, his wife, his secret past! She dressed and went to explore the Vatican, to gaze at the ceiling of the Sistine Chapel until her neck ached, but the more she looked at Michelangelo's figures, the men with their powerful faces and broad muscular torsos, the more she saw Garrett Hamilton. The realisation made her so disgusted with herself that she hurried from the room, intent on eradicating his image from her mind.

She went to sit in a small café and with a decisive gesture took out the notebook she always carried in her bag. Sipping a chocolate-laced capuccino, she set herself to imagining Rome as it would look in the year 2000, a Rome plundered of even the remnants of empire, denuded of all now visible life. But her task was interrupted by a youth who came nonchalantly to share her table, and with a groan of impatience, Clarissa trundled back to the hotel, half of her wishing that a man called Garrett Hamilton had never entered her life, never torn her away from the ardours of her writing desk and its already full enough vistas.

CHAPTER SEVEN

'CLARISSA!' A soft warm bundle bounded into her arms and wrapped its arms around her.

'Ted, you've arrived!' Clarissa lowered the wriggling shape and bent to kiss the little boy. She was surprised at how moved she was to see him.

'Yuck!' Ted wiped her kiss from his mouth. 'That's for grown-ups. This is what I prefer,' and pulling at her head, he rubbed noses with her.

Clarissa laughed, 'I'll remember. Did you have a good flight?'

The question sparked a set of antics which had the entire hotel lobby agape, as Ted, his arms akimbo, raced in circles round the room and made loud engine-like noises.

'That's enough, Ted.' Garrett came up behind him and lifted the squirming little boy into his arms. 'I don't think the people here particularly want a jet landing in their midst!'

Clarissa giggled and he turned two coal black eyes at her and nodded formally, immediately turning his attention back to the child. 'Elinor's just coming down with your coat and then we'll go out for a snack.'

'Is Clarissa coming with us?' Ted asked.

'I think she probably has things she'd rather do,' Garrett replied.

'Do you, Clarissa?' the little boy asked suspiciously, and when Clarissa didn't answer instantly, he looked at his father in triumph. 'There, I told you!'

Garrett shrugged and said with terse politeness, 'Would you like to join us, Clarissa?'

'If it's all right with you,' she nodded.

They went off to the car, and only Elinor and Ted's boundless energy hid the tension between them. Elinor, her soft black eyes glistening, was full of endless 'oohs and aahs' and she kept exclaiming to Clarissa, 'I'm so glad you won that prize and Garrett decided to bring us here.'

The exclamations mounted when, after lunch, they went for a stroll in the Forum and Ted, full of the wonders of Asterix, the indomitable Gaul, made it quite clear to them that the ruins of Rome were all Asterix's doing. Clarissa was grateful for his incessant chatter. Garrett's coldness was beginning to wear her down. She had only known him full of charm or anger, but now, apart from his single question, he hadn't addressed a word directly to her all day and his polite distance was devastating. It took all her energy to treat him in precisely the same way, while her sublimated feelings found some expression in the hugs she could give Ted, the warmth she could show towards Elinor.

When they returned to the hotel, Garrett finally addressed her directly. 'Signor Fiorucci has invited us to his home for dinner this evening. I assumed you would accept—it's only civil. I said we'd be there at eight.' With that he turned and gathering a waving Ted up in his arms, went to his room.

Clarissa followed slowly, feeling like an outcast. She argued with herself that she shouldn't, that this was precisely the way she wanted to be treated by Garret, to treat him. Donning her new misty rose skirt and blouse, she tried to make herself fit for what she imagined would be an elegant household. Signor Fiorucci with his flashing eyes and old-world manners struck her as a man of marked culture. She was suddenly struck by a bout of trembling shyness, and using her brother's voice, she mutely addressed her image, reminding the Clary in the mirror that she was a prize-winning author. For all the good it does me, she thought miserably.

Her instincts about Signor Fiorucci had been correct. The house he inhabited was indeed a palazzo, its baroque portals opening on to a beautifully propor-tioned courtyard, with a sunken pool filled with lush waterlilies at its centre. Then came the entrance proper, through which a small dark man in coat-tails ushered them and then showed them into a vast sitting room.

Clarissa stopped in her tracks. The space was like one she had only ever read about, its frescoed ceilings buttressed by plump cupids, the walls hung with rich oils and the marble floors smooth under her feet. Signor Fiorucci came up to them and smiled at Clarissa's look.

'Welcome, Signorina Harlowe. The home of my ancestors is not quite in the style of your English country houses, but I hope you will enjoy your evening here all the same.' He led them towards a small group of elegant people, sitting in ornate chairs and introduced them to his wife, a vivacious woman with oddly bright red hair; a slender, strikingly attractive young woman with a brooding Botticelli face and a trim young man whose flashing eyes identified him as Signor Fiorucci's son.

Marco immediately engaged Clarissa in conversation. His English was fluent, and it seemed he was an anglophile, his one regret in life being that his studies at Cambridge were over and that now he could only visit England on brief holidays. The chat flowed easily, though Clarissa kept noting out of the corner of her eye that Garrett, dramatically handsome in a dark evening suit, seemed all too intimately at ease with the woman called Alessandra. Trying hard to stifle the jealousy which, despite herself, ached through her, Clarissa focussed her attention on Marco. They were joined by several other people, and when it came to dinner, she found herself between father and son at the opposite end of the table from Garrett. She could see Alessandra had fallen rapidly under his spell, and she suddenly hated him for his easy masculinity. She downed several glasses of wine in nervous succession, and her tongue began to trip lightly over anecdotes about the English countryside, her knack for punning coming to the fore, until she found Marco gazing at her wonderingly and making enough plans to fill a month in Rome.

As they rose from the lavish dining room table to make their way back to the sitting room, Clarissa felt her head swimming and the blood began to drain away from her face.

Garrett was suddenly at her side, his hand scorching her arm. She gazed into his eyes. For a moment he seemed to respond to her look, and then his icy voice cut into her. 'You've been drinking too much and behaving outrageously. I'll take you home just as soon as we've had some coffee, if you can contain yourself for that long.'

'Take your hands off me,' Clarissa muttered between clenched teeth, and then with her last resources, she followed Marco into the next room, responding as best she could to the conversation she now let him lead. Alessandra had sat down at the gleaming grand piano, and as she picked out a light contrapuntal rhythm, Garrett gazed down at her approvingly. Clarissa flinched and accepted the proffered brandy. But as soon as she had drained her second cup of coffee, Garrett was upon her, urging her to her feet, politely bidding the company goodnight. She noticed him holding Alessandra's hand slightly longer than the norm and overheard him say, 'On the Via Veneto, at twelve.'

'Rat!' she fumed irrationally to herself. So he's going to tuck me in safely with the children and then wander off. Two, three, four-timing rat!

The silence between them as they drove to the hotel was so charged that Clarissa thought she would suffocate for sheer lack of air. Garrett didn't make a single comment, and seemed to be so wholly rapt in his own thoughts that she could think of no way of penetrating the hostility which seemed to have settled between them. His rugged profile daunted her in its distance and she would have liked somehow to reintroduce at least a little of the friendly camaraderie which had prevailed on their first day in the city. She realised that it was to a large extent her own fault, but she had no idea of how to go about rectifying the situation without betraying her feelings. So she sat stiffly, as far away from him as she could, taking a little comfort from his tense brow which seemed to signal that he was at least no happier than she was.

But when at the hotel he bade her a polite goodnight,

she could restrain herself no longer and she lashed out at him, 'Go on, go out gallivanting with your women, now that I've served my purpose, won you your prizes!'

His look lacerated her, but he turned away without speaking, and Clarissa went tumbling into bed, wondering whether she could hold out for just those few more days until the prize-giving. Then she would go back to London, she had decided, far from Garrett and the New York which had brought her all this heartache.

When she woke the next day, a bitter taste in her mouth, a dull ache gripping her heart, she realised that she couldn't bear another day of icy coldness in Garrett's company. She would devote the day to looking at pictures. It would quiet her. She dressed quickly and feeling like a fugitive, walked softly down the corridor, hoping against hope that she would bump into neither Ted or Elinor, least of all Garrett himself. She reached the lift and breathed a sigh of relief, only to be confronted by Ted and Elinor as soon as she reached the lobby.

'We're just going to have breakfast,' Ted announced importantly, taking her hand without a question. 'Daddy says I can have some coffee today and look, just look.' He suddenly paused to rummage in Elinor's capacious bag. 'See what I've got!' He dug out a small camera complete with flash and in an instant he had snapped a photograph of Clarissa. 'Dad gave it to me this morning. We're all going to the Colosseum.' He brought out the word without the least effort and took Clarissa's hand again. She knew she didn't have the heart to protest in front of the child, nor Elinor, who equally assumed that she would be coming with them.

Steeling herself against Garrett's arrival, Clarissa sipped her coffee and picked at a roll. When he came, he nodded to her coldly and turned his attention to Ted's endless stream of chatter. He wanted to know about everything, and Clarissa noticed the patient attention Garrett paid to his questions, the serious and informative answers he made. With an attempt at naturalness, he drew Clarissa into the conversation, explaining to Ted that he thought she knew a lot more about feeding Christians to lions than he did, and she was left to embark on a narrative of catacombs and conspiratorial meetings. She caught his eyes once and read a question in them which she wasn't sure she understood. He's probably afraid, she concluded, that I'll do something stupid and embarrass him in front of Ted. She also noticed Elinor looking at her strangely.

'Aren't you hungry, Clarissa?' the girl asked.

Clarissa tried a strained smile. 'I had too much last night.'

'You look pale, the girl noted. 'Perhaps you'd like to rest today.'

'No,' Ted was emphatic, 'Clarissa has to come with us and be one of the lions in the circus.' With his usual quickness, he brought out a pencil and sketched a picture on a paper napkin and passed it to Clarissa. 'That's you as a lion,' he said.

Clarissa smiled weakly. And that, she thought, was that.

They drove to the Colosseum and walked through one of its many entrances into the main circus. Clarissa was amazed at its scale. Somehow she had imagined a small amphitheatre. Ted was ecstatic, storming about, creating games which involved all of them climbing up into the stalls and racing down at him from behind to take him by surprise. On one of these gargantuan attacks, Clarissa stumbled, and Garrett stretched out his arms to catch her. She fellt against him, then pulled away as if scorched.

Ted watched her strangely and took his father's hand. 'Don't you like my dad any more, Clarissa?'

Clarissa flushed hotly. 'Yes, yes, of course I do,' she stammered.

The little boy looked out at her from under his dark fringe of hair, his eyes unblinking in the soft face. Then he turned away, suddenly quiet, as if the spirit of play had gone out of him. Clarissa went up to him and ruffled his hair. 'I like you as well, very much,' she said, trying to keep the tears away from her eyes.

Garrett gathered the child up in his arms. 'Come on, we're going to go off to Ostia Antica now, while the weather holds. We can have a picnic out on the ruins of the city. Perhaps Clarissa would like to drive and I can tell you some stories.' He threw her a stern look and tried to cheer Ted along.

'I don't think I can,' Clarissa apologised. 'I haven't driven for months, and it's the wrong side of the road.'

'Right, then you're responsible for stories.'

'I'm a little better at those,' Clarissa acquiesced wryly, and settling herself in the back seat with the little boy, still solemn, huddled against her, she began a long rambling narrative set in the time of the Romans, which she spun from heaven knows what sources. The story went on for as long as the drive, and by the time they arrived, both Ted and Elinor and Garrett had become ancient Romans, despite Ted's protests that he was a Gaul, and she had somehow become a Carthaginian.

They trekked through the ruins of the antique port, its lines laid out on a grid almost as rigorous as New York's Clarissa thought, looked at innumerable archaeological remains, bought ancient pitchers and tiny figurines. Remembering the present she had meant to buy for Garrett on their first day in the city, Clarissa splurged on a small, beautifully wrought clay dog, its parts all still intact, and presented it to Ted. She kept well apart from Garrett, knowing that if the lines of tension between them became any more taut, they must needs break. When she looked at him surreptitiously, she could see these very lines etched in his face. His eyes, unless he turned them on his son, were bleak, and she knew that her own face must reflect the same forces. The business of being polite, indeed appearing happy and carefree, seemed to be adding years to them in minutes.

They went off to have dinner in a homely little fish restaurant, the Villa dei Pescatori, in which the large, smiling hostess plied them with food and drink, taking Ted on her lap and making him repeat basic Italian phrases, insisting on calling Clarissa his beautiful young mother and treating Garrett as if he were some returning hero. In the midst of all this good will, Clarissa could feel some of the tensions of the last week easing, and when they returned to the car she offered to drive if Garrett wanted her to and promised to navigate. It was dark now and Ted and Elinor, tucked safely in the back seat, seemed to go instantly off to sleep. They drove in silence for some miles, Clarissa concentrating carefully on the road, and at last feeling somewhat easier behind the wheel, as the automatic responded willingly to her every gesture.

Suddenly Garrett's voice, hoarse as if from unuse, cracked the silence. 'I wish you'd stop treating me like some leper, Clarissa, some leper who might infect you with vile sin. Even Ted has noticed.'

She swallowed painfully. 'I don't like being played with.'

He didn't seem to have heard her and his voice rolled on. 'You keep throwing my attachment—presumably with Bianca—in my face at every turn. I don't live with Bianca, just in case you hadn't noticed in your dreamy writer's abstraction. Though I can't deny that we've had our days. I'm not a newborn lamb, as you may have gathered.' His tone rose a notch and grew harder, edged with pain. 'I don't live with anyone except Ted, who's my prime responsibility, my primary care. I won't have any woman hurting him any more than he may already have been hurt.'

Clarissa took this in with a stirring of guilt, but it only sharpened the edge of her own ache.

'And that's why you tolerate me, is it? Because Ted for some mysterious reason of his own, seems to like me?' Her voice trembled.

Suddenly he chuckled. 'That's exactly right. That's why I tolerate you, with your moods, your ferocious tongue, your spirited, prickly sense of yourself, all of it. You make a good mother.'

She didn't know whether he was mocking her outright, but his tone made her rage. 'Yes, a good child-minder. You could pay me a fee,' her voice rose sharply. 'Then there's the other reason for tolerance. I make it easy for you to win bets,' she hissed at him. 'Gullible little me, quickly obeying your orders helps to make you probably the only publisher in America who can keep his serious fiction list alive!' She turned to glare at him, swerving the car in the process.

'What are you talking about, Clarissa?' She could feel his eyes boring into her.

'You know very well what I'm talking about! Didn't you take up a bet, whisk your little finger through a catalogue to land at random on me, not *too* hideous me, and say "That one—that one will suffer marketing and promotion and lessons in love",' her voice cracked, but she persisted, 'and prove to all and sundry that if you package and sell something, anything, properly, it'll win you the race.'

'Who told you all this, Clarissa?' His voice was icy and cut through her rising tide of hysteria.

'Bianca,' she said quietly, adding, 'your lovely, loyal mistress, Bianca, who knows all about the marketing and promotion of life!' She was near to tears, and angrily she slammed her foot down on the accelerator.

'Slow down, Clarissa,' Garrett said harshly, 'and listen—listen carefully. If you were in my place, wouldn't you take any chance you could, any opportunity to save a fiction list, to prove that it could work if the right effort went into it? We're not talking about one book, one writer, but many. And a principle, as well. If we live in a world of packages and promotion, then we might as well use those tools on something valuable. Not simply say, it can't work: the public—that vast anonymous body to be used to back up anybody's statistics—doesn't want anything good. That's nonsense. So I tried. I don't know if we've won the race yet. And I'm sorry, given the way you seem to resent all this, that the lottery picked you.' His voice sounded strained, tired, but Clarissa couldn't admit he might be right.

'All that doesn't belie the fact that you've manipulated me, used me blatantly—you with your lessons in love.

And showing Bianca all those original notes which were stolen; telling her about how my book needed more sexual tension; laughing with her about me. It's hideous, it's indecent!' her tone rose. 'I thought you cared!' Her voice was strangled by a rising sob, and suddenly she saw a small furry body run across the car's path and she veered aggressively round it. Then the lights of an oncoming car beamed down on her with terrifying speed, and in a panic-stricken flash, she knew that impact was imminent. Oh, my God, oh, my God! she thought. With my selfish stupidity, I'm going to kill us all!

And that was all she knew until she woke with a sense of horror to see floodlights blinding her, strange voices shouting and a man in a white coat prodding her limbs. Instantly she remembered, and with a cry which she thought must rend her in two, she screamed, screamed so that her throat burned and her mouth grew rigid on the words, repeated over and over again, 'Garrett, Ted, Elinor!'

When he appeared at her side, his face haggard, glowing eerily in the floodlights, and bent in the moist grass to plant soft, soothing kisses on her face, she knew that she must have dreamt him. But her arms that flew round him seemed to be touching hard flesh and as he whispered in her ear, 'Darling, my darling, it's all right,' and her fingers traced his remembered features, Clarissa realised that he was solidly there. She clung to him, afraid now to look into his face, to pose the dreaded question.

'Ted?' she brought out at last, her mouth forming the word, though she could hear no sound.

'He's all right, my darling—not a scratch. Elinor too.'

A deep aching sigh escaped her. 'Thank God!' she breathed.

Garrett stroked her hair, his breath cool on her forehead. 'We're all miraculously alive and well. Even the driver in the other car. You turned away just at the right moment, so it wasn't head-on.'

She looked at him more closely now, that beloved

face dramatically etched in the odd night-time light and she could see a deep jagged scratch at his temple. She fingered it gently.

'Just some glass,' he shrugged her silent query away. 'The cars are in far worse shape than we are. And you, my young lady,' he looked at her tenderly, 'are the one we've all been worried about. They tell me there's nothing broken, but you did take a little while to wake up. It must be the shock of talking honestly to me at last.' He smiled at her tenderly and then kissed her again before she was lifted off the ground on a stretcher, placed into an ambulance, despite her protests that she was perfectly all right, and after some loud-voiced arguments, found herself surrounded not only by a white-clothed attendant, but an excited Ted, a worried Elinor, and Garrett himself, clutching her hand as if he had no intention of letting it go.

As Clarissa watched the faces around her in the dim light of the ambulance interior, tears suddenly began to pour from her eyes. Through her own stupidity she had almost destroyed them all, obliterated the very beings it was now so painfully clear to her she deeply loved. She breathed a silent prayer of thanks to whatever being might watch over her; and oblivious to the dull ache in her limbs, she stretched to take Ted's small hand and rumple his hair. He looked at her, his eyes vaster than his face, and despite his father's admonishments started to talk again excitedly. 'A *real* crash, Clarissa—a real one. Great! Just like on the television,' and his hands went into high speed action while he mimicked the noise of the car. She knew he must be in a state of shock.

'Hush!' Elinor and Garrett both stilled his voice, as Clarissa hugged the little body. Over its warmth she met Garrett's eyes, her own swimming with tears, and the look she saw there made her heart race. The attendant ordered her to lie quietly and she tried to relax into the stiff fabric of the stretcher. But as soon as she lowered what were indeed heavy lids, the nightmare of the impending impact returned, the lights of an oncoming car beamed down on her with unstoppable speed, and her eyes jolted open in panic. Garrett took in her expression and caressing her hand, whispered consolingly, but it was no use. Every time Clarissa closed her eyes it was the same, the same nightmare vision, and each time she opened them, a sob of relief escaped her at the sight of her companions. She clung to Garrett's hand as if it were a lifeline, and only when they had reached the small suburban hospital and she was wheeled off did she unwillingly let go.

After another round of examinations had been completed in a surprisingly quiet emergency ward, Clarissa was taken off to a sienna-tinted room. Garrett, hurrying back and forth between her and the other two, explained that, some painful bruising aside, she was all right, but they wanted to keep her under observation for a day.

'I shall have to leave you here for a while to tend to Ted and Elinor,' he said softly, his eyes worrying over her.

'I'll be fine,' she consoled him, hiding the twinge of fear she felt at being alone. She was sure her gaze must reflect her love, as he bent over to kiss her lightly, as her hand rose of its own accord to touch the jagged cut on his brow. 'Take care of yourself!' she called after him.

Try as she might, Clarissa couldn't sleep. Her eyes open to the darkness, she kept reliving the accident and tried to make sense of the reality Garrett's words and the subsequent collision had thrust in her face. Step by step, as her eyes flicked over the few objects in the simple room, she went over her relationship with Garrett, seeing for the first time the care he had lavished on her; his patience in the face of her taunts and merciless criticism of his work tactics. And even if she put her original interpretation on the past, did any of that, even Bianca, really matter, as long as he cared for Clarissa now? God, how she longed for him; how she loved him! The proximity of death, of total loss, had a way of erasing nuances, of simplifying matters.

At last she fell into a heavy drugged sleep, filled with terrifying dreams in which she was herself, yet in Ted or Elinor's body, watching a headstrong, irritable woman driving them all to disaster. She woke in a sweat to find Garrett's eyes, sea-blue in the clear morning light, looking down on her. 'Ted?' It was the first word which rose to her lips.

'He's calm now,' Garrett's deep voice consoled her. 'Elinor's well too, though a little more fragile than yesterday, when she was busy coping.'

Clarissa smiled and sat up stiffly in the bed.

'Sore?' Garrett asked, his eyes betraying his concern.

'A little,' she admitted. 'And you?' He looked haggard, his face gaunt from lack of sleep.

He took her hand. 'I'm blissfully happy.'

'Yes,' she murmured, a question in her eyes. 'Everything seems simple after one's skirted death.'

He nodded.

A pretty young nurse walked in with Ted. She exchanged some words in Italian with Garrett and left to return within minutes carrying a large pad and some crayons. Ted's solemn eyes lit up.

'I'm going to draw lots of car crashes,' he announced, settling himself on the floor. Garrett and Clarissa watched him silently, and it seemed to Clarissa that a light-filled dome had descended on the three of them, encasing them in a tremulous peace.

After another round of examinations, they were free to leave, and they returned to the hotel for a quiet dinner. Over the food, Garrett coached Clarissa in a few Italian phrases which would come in handy at the prize-giving ceremony the following evening.

'I want you word-perfect, Miss Harlowe. The cameras will be present,' he teased her. 'And you wouldn't want to let me down now.'

'*Vi ringrazio molto per questo onore . . .*' Clarissa repeated carefully, and Ted echoed her.

Elinor laughed. 'You both have dreadful accents!'

'I'm doing my best,' Clarissa insisted, feeling a twinge

of nervousness rising in her. In her present mood, she would dearly have loved to forget the whole thing.

'They'll be pleased to hear you say anything in Italian, no matter how simple,' Garrett encouraged her. 'In any case, you'll be wonderful. You know,' he looked at her reflectively and then laughed, 'you're distinctly a Clarissa Harlowe with a difference. A victim who survives everything: burglaries, collisions, prize-givings, even me!'

She met his laughing eyes intently for a long moment, took in the rugged planes of his face. 'I'm not too sure I've survived the last yet,' she said.

They retired early, Garrett leaving Clarissa with a soft kiss and an apology, 'I should stay with Ted tonight, and you need to rest.'

She nodded. His touch made her nerve ends tingle, filled her with a warm sense of anticipation. Yet as soon as she was alone, a nagging anxiety rose in her, breaking her peace. After the prize-giving ceremony, what would happen? She had read in Garrett's eyes that he cared for her—but he had said nothing, made no promises. Perhaps these last dramatic hours had only fostered an illusion in her, a one-sided unfulfillable hope. And once she had served her purpose, completed her task, it would all be over.

The anxiety ate at her throughout the night and the next day, which they spent walking quietly in the magnificent Borghese Gardens or simply resting. Ted made a great many more drawings. At one point Clarissa heard him ask Elinor, 'Do you think Laura would like these?'

Clarissa caught her breath, her deeply rooted insecurity rising again to the fore. Here was another unknown factor she hadn't yet contended with: Garrett's wife and her inevitable legacy. How had that experience marked him? Might he never want to share his life fully with another woman again?

By the time evening arrived and he had still not said anything about what tomorrow might bring, Clarissa could feel that she was beginning to steel herself against him, against the possibility of more pain. She resolved that after the prize-giving, she would tell him that she was going back to England. Then, if he really wanted her, he would have to make it clear, offer some sign.

She dressed carefully, forcing herself to pay attention to her appearance. The chic black dress, bought specially for this occasion, was so beautiful that its very feel on her skin lightened her mood a little. She made herself up carefully, noting that her pallor gave a touch of mystery to her face and the play of emotions in her haunted her eyes, made them larger than life. When the telephone rang to announce Marco—who commiserated with her over the accident and offered to pick them up and drive them to the ceremony—she accepted happily. Perhaps Garrett needed to know that other men found her attractive, interesting... She scolded herself for resorting to ploys, but smiled nonetheless.

Under Garrett's door she tucked a note saying she would meet him in the bar. Then she went downstairs to wait for Marco. He arrived almost instantly and his flashing eyes flattered her, as he ordered a celebratory drink.

'Not too much,' Clarissa laughed, 'or I shall forget my prepared speech!' She recounted the story of the last twenty-four hours to him, only suddenly to be aware of a pair of eyes burning into her nape. She swallowed hard as Garrett came into view, and though he greeted Marco graciously, the glance he gave Clarissa was black with disapproval. Serves you right, she thought childishly to herself as she answered his polite enquiry about how she felt.

Cameras flashed when Clarissa, Marco and Garrett were announced in the sumptuous hall where the prize-giving ceremony was to take place. As her eyes recovered from the glare, Clarissa made out a stately room with gilded ceilings and portrait-filled walls. Elegantly dressed people milled round in small groups. Marco played host, introducing them to youthful and ageing luminaries. Separated from Garrett by the crowd, Clarissa clung to Marco's arm. Her practised speech seemed to have totally escaped her mind and she tried to remember the words, as she moved from group to group. But they wouldn't come, and she looked round the room for Garrett, spying him in conversation with Signor Fiorucci. The sight of his proudly erect carriage, the striking face with its brooding, intelligent eyes, suddenly made her pulses race. She walked towards him nervously and when his eyes turned on her, she felt a tremor run through her.

'I've forgotten my lines,' she whispered in his ear.

He gave her arm a comforting squeeze and repeated the words for her, just as a hush fell over the room. Clarissa waited anxiously until her name was called by a bearded elderly man who was the head of the writers' academy. Then, bringing her acting talents to life, she walked slowly up to the platform. The audience below her gazed at her expectantly, and suddenly the remembered words flew out of her mouth, and more too, a little impromptu speech in English in which she tremulously thanked her Italian publishers as well as Garrett Hamilton—her voice paused around his name—for all the help they had given her. She hoped her future work would live up to the present honour.

Then it was time for dinner and Clarissa, her face flushed, her legs wobbly, was led to another room where the array of silver and dazzling chandeliers made her feel quite dizzy. She found herself at a head table, a grey-haired dignitary at either side, and she looked round for Garrett, taking support from his eyes when she found them, only to note that he was sitting next to the beautiful Alessandra. The now recognisable spike of jealousy fractured her, making her halt wildly in mid-sentence. Throwing her shoulders back, Clarissa chided herself severely. It was ludicrous for her to go through one of the more important moments of her life feeling like a silly aggrieved woman whose sole interest was a male. With that contemptible self-image to spur her on, she launched herself into conversation again with her table partners. And when Garrett came to claim her at the dinner's end, she was pleased to find that she hadn't thought of him for at least an hour. She smiled a little smile of self-congratulation.

But sitting next to him in the taxi on the way back to the hotel, she knew that she had merely been play-acting. The realisation that she would gladly have done without the prize only to hear Garrett say he cared for her made her shiver. She really was very far gone.

'Cold, Clarissa?' Garrett's arm wove its way round her shoulders and the sheer charge it brought, even through the thickness of her coat, made her tremble in fear. He held her more closely to him and turning her face towards his, he looked at her deeply. 'Well done, madame writer,' a smile curved his mobile lips. 'My random choice among Jethrop authors marked my lucky day.' His eyes held a mocking light. 'Perhaps I should let chance determine more of my life.'

'You seem to do quite well whatever determines your life,' Clarissa's tone held a sting.

He looked down at her curiously, as if he were judging her mood and then, his own voice mildly acerbic, countered, 'You don't seem to do so badly yourself, Clarissa.'

'What do you know about it?' she thrust at him, suddenly angry at herself, angry at him, angry at the hectic trajectory of her recent life which had shown her that there seemed to be no peace to be found anywhere except near him, and perhaps not even there. She pulled away from beneath his arm to the farther corner of the car seat and huddled into it.

'I guess I know less than I thought.' His eyes sparkled darkly in the light of passing street lamps, and with a shrug, he took a cigarette from his coat pocket and inhaled deeply. A fraught silence settled between them which Clarissa desperately wanted to break, but the only words which played in her mind were that she loved him, and that was the one thing she couldn't bring herself to reveal.

And tomorrow? By tomorrow it would all be over. Their reasons for being together were gone. She had received her prize, fulfilled her use, and now it was time to take up the strings of her own life.

At the door to her room she turned to meet his eyes at last. 'I guess this is goodbye,' she said, a tremor in her voice.

'What are you talking about, Clarissa?' He looked at her strangely, his nostrils flaring.

She shrugged. 'I've done my bit. I'm off tomorrow.'

With barely controlled irritation, Garrett took her key from her hand and opened her door, striding into the room after her. Then, as if the privacy of the space allowed him to give vent to his feelings, his voice cut into her. 'Stop behaving like a child, Clarissa! You're not going anywhere in your present state and certainly not alone.'

The fact that his words comprised an order made her want to defy him instantly. 'Why ever not? I've . . .'

'Clarissa,' her name emerged huskily from his lips. 'Clarissa, stop this!' With one step he was next to her, his hands on her shoulders as if he were about to shake her, and then his mouth came crashing down on hers with an intensity that made her heart pound madly. She drank in his kiss as if her throat had been parched from an eternity of waiting and her arms wove round him, clinging to his taut back, roving to caress the tangle of his thick hair.

'Why must you always fight me, Clarissa?' he murmured in her ear, his breath vibrating through her so that she could feel the charge of his voice resonating in her limbs. 'We're so good together when we're like this. We could be so *very* good together.' He pulled her down beside him on the edge of the bed, his lips nuzzling her nape, seeking out the bare skin of her throat, sending tendrils of flame through her body, so that she arched against him, all of her kindled into a single life, her tortuous cerebrations for once at rest. With a gentle hand Garrett undid the tiny buttons of her dress and his lips pressed softly against her breast.

She could feel a fluid warmth pulsing deep inside her, and when his lips found hers again, wave after molten wave enveloped her, so that she pulled him down with her on the bed, wanting to feel the hard lines of his body etched on hers. A low moan escaped him, and then as his fingers touched the painful ribs above her waist and she flinched, he drew away slightly and with a featherlight touch stroked the contours of her face. 'We mustn't tonight, darling,' his voice seemed to Clarissa to come from some distant point in space. 'I'll hurt you. Just another day or two.'

Her eyes fluttered open to take in the drama of his face, the slightly wry curve of the mobile lips, the dark skin beneath the storm of white hair, and she drew close to him, not wanting even the shadow of distance to separate them.

He chucked her playfully under the chin and with one supple movement he was by the telephone, ordering drinks to be brought to the room. 'Make yourself decent, woman,' he commanded, his eyes raking her reclining form with a hint of devilry. 'This is a family hotel!'

Not quite so swift in her change of mood, Clarissa looked out at him from wide amber eyes and he laughed, bending to kiss her lightly on the lips.

'I'm scheming, scheming beautifully. Tomorrow, if you're up to it, we shall go off to Venice, stopping place of all the best literary ladies and their ardent lovers, and there . . .' his eyes spoke the rest of his thought. 'Would you like that Clarissa?'

Suddenly she caught his mood and with a mischievous sparkle in her eye, she nodded slowly. 'As long as I don't have to be called George!'

'Dreadful name,' he muttered. 'No,' his dark eyes turned on her enveloping her in a palpable embrace, 'Clarissa will do. Clarissa Harlowe will just about do.'

CHAPTER EIGHT

As the *vaporetto* chugged slowly along the canal Clarrisa felt that her mouth had dropped open in a permanent state of wonder. Even the rambunctious Ted whose hand lay warmly in hers seemed to have been silenced by the magic of the spectacle unfolding before them: a sky fretted with every kind of pinnacle imaginable—from great domes to spires to the arabesque of minarets—all clearly etched in a pale, strangely luminous light. There was a soft clarity to the atmosphere, a palpable sense of the city having been caught somewhere out of time in a space where horizons ceased to exist as pale blue water and limpid sky mingled together.

Feeling Garrett's gaze on her, Clarissa met his eyes. 'I think I need to be pinched,' she said softly. 'It can't all really exist.'

He chuckled, his eyes softened by a glow which seemed to come as much from the atmosphere as from him. 'I'm ready to oblige any time,' he draped his arm casually round her and pinched her gently. But his touch, Clarissa noted, did nothing to dispel her sense of wonder; indeed, if anything, it increased it. From nowhere, some lines of Shelley's dropped into her mind.

> *I leaned and saw the city, and could mark*
> *How from their many isles, in evening's gleam,*
> *Its temples and its palaces did seem*
> *Like fabrics of enchantment piled to heaven.*

As their small party trooped off the boat into the gracious elegance of the hotel on the Grand Canal, the fabric of enchantment persisted. Somewhere in the recesses of herself Clarissa knew that the fabric was woven out of the taut threads which pulled her magnetically towards Garrett. To this the city added a rich pattern of rococo embroidery. In a rush of pure joy, she saw Garrett striding back from the reception desk, and needing to give expression to the surge of feeling, she lifted Ted into her arms and hugged him tightly. 'Better than Disneyland, isn't it?' she teased him.

He looked at her seriously and nodded, adding, 'But there aren't any strange animals.'

'Oh, I don't know,' Clarissa laughed. 'Just imagine St Mark's in the moonlight: a meeting of giant tortoises, and the *campanile* is like nothing so much as a giraffe.'

Ted smiled and squirmed out of her arms, only to announce to his approaching father and Elinor, 'Clarissa says St Mark's is like a lot of giant tortoises.'

Garrett looked from Clarissa to his son, and the warmth of the expression on his face made her swallow hard. 'Primordial creatures emerging from the depths of the lagoon, why not?'

As they went to their rooms, he explained to Ted how Venice had literally risen from a lagoon, how the great houses were built on wooden piles hammered through its mud to the firm blue clay eighteen feet below the surface. 'We're on a little island now, one of over a hundred.'

'Like Manhattan,' Ted remarked, a note of triumph in his voice.

Clarissa smiled, and with a wave to the threesome as they reached her room announced that she for one would be ready in five minutes for a stroll around the Piazza San Marco. Not a moment was to be wasted if they were to catch it in the soft afternoon light.

She slipped into her room, pausing to take in its magnificent proportions, the tall windows which opened on to the lagoon and from there the sea; the ornately carved old furniture and moulded ceilings. She sighed. She had woken this morning feeling as if she were in a state of grace, and the radiance in her eyes, the smile which played round her lips as she glimpsed herself in the mirror, spoke of its continued existence. As if she had risen newly born from the ashes of the collision, the initial stiffness now gone from her joints; a

tremulous happiness, rekindled each time she met the
glow in Garrett's eyes, visible in each of her movements.
Even the reviews of her book, which she had at last
read properly all in a bunch on the brief flight from
Rome, hadn't dented the feeling of grace. It was as if all
that had to do with another woman, another time, one
quite remote from this present which was totally
bounded by the magic circle around the man who went
by the name of Garrett Hamilton and herself.

Clarissa knocked shyly at his door. 'I'm ready,' she
called. He stepped back for her to enter and she took in
the crispness of the fresh shirt which moulded his broad
shoulders, the half-knotted tie and above it the dazzle
of his eyes in the strong face. He pulled her towards
him and for a brief, tantalising moment she felt kisses
raining on her face and her lips. Then he drew away, a
devilish smile lighting his face as his look caressed her.
He reached for the jacket which he had flung on his bed
and ushered her out of the room.

'Mustn't keep the family—or the Piazza San
Marco—waiting,' he grinned.

The four of them strolled along the marble
chequerboarding of the square, banked by the two
residences of the historic Procurators, towards the
fantastic façade of St Mark's with its multitude of
pillars and white domes. It seemed to Clarissa akin to a
gigantic treasure trove, partly of gold, opal, mother-of-
pearl, its great vaulted porches replete with mosaics and
sculpture—birds fluttering among branches, an endless
network of buds, plumes and angels which made one
feel that the eye could easily rove there for a blissful
eternity.

But Ted was ready for the promised *granita*, and in
the dying light of the afternoon, they went to Florian's
and sat listening to the musicians while Ted and Elinor
gorged themselves on a variety of quite undinnerlike
delicacies.

'You'll never go to a Macdonald's again,' Elinor
teased the little boy as she revelled in the marvels of a
honeycombed ice.

'And once I've fed Clarissa this evening,' Garrett's eyes flickered over her, 'she'll even give up the wonders of roast beef and Yorkshire pudding!'

'Don't forget fish and chips,' Clarissa laughed. 'I could never give up both.'

'Never?' Garrett asked, mocking her lightly, though his eyes posed a different question.

When they had finished they strolled through a darkening maze of alleys, bought some obligatory postcards—one of which Clarissa immediately sent off to her brother—and returned to the hotel to tuck a recalcitrant Ted into bed. 'Only if you tell me a fabulous story about Venice,' the little boy challenged, and interrupting a stern order from Garrett, Clarissa said she had just the one.

The little boy smiled triumphantly. 'I am glad you and Clarissa like each other again, even though she smashed the car,' he announced to his father.

Garrett cuffed him playfully. 'Into bed, smart aleck! And don't wear Clarissa out.'

After Clarissa's tale had woven its way to the end of a first instalment, she went to her room with a sense of mounting excitement. It was the first time she and Garrett were to be properly alone since the previous evening, and as she showered and dressed, she was suddenly struck by a sense of the fragility of what now existed between them, like one of those wonderful objects of fluted glass she had spied in the arcades, which needed to be handled delicately, amost reverentially.

When he came to her door, she looked at his tall, darkly clad frame shyly, half afraid to meet his eyes and what she read there, and as he took her arm she trembled slightly feeling the mark of each finger on her skin.

They walked, Clarissa wasn't sure in what direction, through innumerable narrow lanes, banked by handsome, sometimes dilapidated buildings which seemed to meet over their heads. Holding hands, they crossed bridges, each one more beautiful than the last, meandered through tiny squares which came upon them by surprise. Words seemed unnecessary, somehow too prosaic for the magic which the city exuded and the feelings which enveloped them, and it was only when they had passed through an unostentatious façade into a restaurant composed of a series of intimate arched enclaves that speech returned.

Garrett looked at her seriously, his eyes flickering darkly in the candlelight. 'You don't mind having Ted and Elinor here with us, Clarissa? he asked hesitantly. 'It's not every woman's idea of a Venetian idyll.'

She gazed at him, wondering that he couldn't see her contentment, wondering if she had been impatient in any of her gestures. She shook her head slowly. 'It's more of an idyll than I ever imagined.'

'Perhaps I'm a little too careful about Ted,' he offered after a moment, 'but—well,' he seemed to be about to say something and then changed his mind, 'it's just that I don't like to leave him on his own for too long.'

Of its own accord, Clarissa's hand rose to smooth the furrow in his brow. He brought her fingers to his lips and kissed them softly one by one. Something inside her moved darkly and he smiled, a slow, steady smile that irradiated his features.

A white-shirted waiter approached them with menus. Garrett glimpsed at the list. 'The food here used to be superb.'

'When were you last here?' she asked, needing to know him.

A muscle moved tensely in his jaw. 'Some years ago. With my wife.'

'Were you very much in love with her?' Clarissa asked, wishing she hadn't as she saw his face darkening.

At last he said, 'We'll talk about that some other time, Clarissa. There's enough that I have to tell you tonight.'

She looked at him expectantly, half of her afraid of what might be coming.

'But let's eat first,' he smiled, taking her hand again.

A series of intricately flavoured dishes passed in front of them, accompanied by full-bodied wines, and as they ate, Clarissa found that again it was she who was being drawn out, about her plans, her new book.

'And have you forgiven me for having placed a bet on your head?' Garrett asked her suddenly.

A low laugh broke from her. 'One writer in the service of many... Mr Hamilton, you put very convincing arguments for your case, despite the fact that they seemed to take me on a collision course. Of course I forgive you,' she added, meeting his eyes.

He didn't smile, only asked in a slightly husky voice, 'And do you think, Clarissa, you could forgive one more horror I've inadvertently involved you in?'

She glanced at him questioningly, knowing in her heart that nothing in him seemed beyond her forgiveness. Yet his expression made her anxious.

'Do you remember,' he asked, gazing at her intently, 'just before the accident, you accused me of having told Bianca about what you call our lessons in love, having shown her the notes I prepared for your manuscript?'

Clarissa paled, not wanting to summon the agony of that moment. But she nodded.

'I want you to know that I didn't. I couldn't have. Whatever else I may be, I'm not that kind of a heel.'

She met his eyes, believing him. 'But then how did she know? I didn't dream what she said.'

He shrugged. 'I wondered too. I rang her, pressed her on it.' A sombre look clouded his face so that Clarissa imagined the storm that must have passed between them. 'I don't know how, what possessed her, but she engineered the burglary in your loft.'

Clarissa's mouth dropped. He took her hand and stroked it gently. 'It's terrible, frightful, but I'm partly to blame. She was jealous of you, insanely jealous of the attention I was paying you, and I hadn't noticed the full extent of it. Hell hath no fury...' A sad smile twisted his features.

'But you said, you implied...' Clarissa felt a knot

tightening in her stomach. 'You implied it was finished between you.'

'It was over between us a long time ago,' he shrugged. 'But we work together, see each other . . . and these things, feelings, aren't always equal on all sides. And to her credit, Bianca didn't know that you'd been knocked out. She just wanted to get her hands on the manuscript, to prevent you from coming with me to Frankfurt.'

The knot in Clarissa's stomach grew larger. So many excuses for Bianca . . .

'Do you still care for her very much?' she asked simply.

He looked at her quietly. 'I've never loved Bianca, if that's what you mean, Clarissa; but as I think we've agreed, attachments come in many guises. I've never pretended to be a saint.'

She fingered her napkin nervously, wanting to ask him what kind of attachment he had with her. Then, feeling his gaze on her skin, she met his eyes, only to find herself swimming in their depths.

'She was right to be jealous, Clarissa,' Garrett said huskily, taking her hand. 'Shall we go?'

She nodded and followed him towards a small pier where they climbed into a gondola, its high prow richly bright against the sleek darkness of its body.

'It's like someone else's life. A dream,' Clarissa murmured, watching the waters stream past them, the crescent moon which played between the buildings and left a shimmering trail in its reflected wake. His arms enveloped her, held her close.

She felt, as he guided her towards his room, that she was in a trance, occasioned as much by the broodingly handsome man at her side, as by the city's magic. And as she stood on the terrace gazing at the flickering lights in the lagoon, she wondered at the city's enchantment, the forces which it conjured up within the self which had led some, she remembered, to fling themselves into these very waters. Before these ominous images could unfold within her, she felt Garrett behind her, his

strong arms encircling her as he nipped little circles of
flame into the bare skin of her neck. She turned in the
fold of his arms, the silk of her suit swishing against the
rougher texture of his, and caught the smouldering fire
of his gaze as his lips pressed down on hers, probing her
mouth so that she could feel the blood begin to course
wildly through her veins, set up a pounding in her head.
Behind its din, she heard a muted knocking at the door.
With a low groan Garrett turned from her.

Clarissa made for the nearest chair and sank into it,
blindly watching the black-suited waiter deposit a silver
ice bucket and a bottle of champagne on the ornately
carved table before her. Without focussing her eyes on
him, she was intensely aware of Garrett's movements,
the politeness with which he thanked the man, the lithe
precision of his gestures as he uncorked the bottle; and
filling their glasses to the brim, brought one to her lips,
beckoning her to drink. His eyes gazed at her with a
dark desire, and suddenly she was afraid. She stood up,
as if to leave.

'Clarissa!' His voice stopped her, held a threat as well
as a question. He pulled her towards him, holding her
so tightly that she was imprisoned against him. 'We
can't keep up the present pattern of this dance for ever.'
His eyes were edged with pain and his mouth wrenched
down on hers so that his skin was rough on her face
and she could feel the pulsing of his hard body through
the skein of their clothes.

A little cry escaped her.

'I'm sorry, my darling, but I can't let you go. Not
now.' He held her to him more gently, but his kiss was
urgent, pressing, and her arms rose to embrace him of
their own accord, seeking out the bare skin of his neck,
the smoothness of his shoulders beneath his shirt.

Their eyes locked and Clarissa could feel something
darkly immutable pass between them. With a terrible
suddenness, a primal awareness, she knew that Garrett
meant more to her than any daylight self which spoke
of reserve, of inhibitions, of chastity.

'Come,' he whispered, and with a single movement he

lifted her on to the bed with its soft white coverlet. His
lips sought hers again, while with a deft caressing touch
his hands explored the soft curves of her body, so that
she thrilled to him, wanting to feel him even
closer, wanting the sense of his skin against hers.

As he lifted the delicate camisole over her head and
she lay bare to his gaze, she saw her own desire
reflected in the smouldering of his eyes. With an infinite
gentleness, he stroked her, his fingers and lips waking
her secret skin into a sensitivity so acute that she arched
against him with a passion which was akin to an ache.
'Beautiful, so beautiful,' he murmured, his breath
hoarse in her ear. Slowly he undressed her, his hands
cherishing her, smoothing the satin of her skin,
arousing sensations in her she had never before
experienced. Shedding his own clothes, he guided her
hands down the taut lines of his body, the hard thighs
entwined with hers. She felt him shudder under her
touch and a warm tide rose through her veins,
enveloping her, obliterating everything in her except the
blissful rain of his kisses, the exquisite sense of skin on
skin. His body flexed against her, his breath hoarse in
her ear and she moaned, a little animal sound, as
somewhere in her an inevitable rhythm rose, arched,
flowed to meet his.

Through the mounting swell of her passion she heard
his voice calling her name, and she opened her eyes to
see his face etched in the moonlight above hers. Her
hands rose to his hair and she fingered its rough tangle,
breathed in the moist male smell of him, a ferny breath
of the outdoors. In his eyes, she glimpsed an urgency, a
deep tenderness, and her heart turned over. His lips
mouthed a question. 'May I, Clarissa, now—please?'
and she answered by seeking out his mouth, fiercely
wanting him, her womb stirring with a new yearning.

Gently, gently, he touched her, arcing against her
with his hardness, and he let out a hoarse cry, as if of
surprise. His breath came hard, 'My darling, my
darling,' he moaned, and with a dark pulsing passion,
he entered her. A shaft of pain seared through her,

timeless yet endless, forming her lips into his name, and then slowly waves of unknown pleasure lapped within her, rising, mounting, carrying her off into a rhythmic rapture of sound, an ocean of sense which made them as one.

When she opened her eyes to him, his own were glowing down on her. He caressed the moist hair from her forehead; his limbs still entwined with hers, he leaned his head on an elbow and gazed at her.

Clarissa smiled, a wide languorous smile. 'So that's what it's all about,' she said, the trembling humour in her voice, barely disguising the depth of her feeling.

He stroked her gently, letting his fingers skim her moist skin.

'That's only the beginning of what it's about.' His look taunted her, shy of their mutual passion, and then grew serious. His voice wondered at her, caressed her, as he fingered the crumpled sheet, and their eyes focussed simultaneously on a bright spot of red. 'I didn't realise until . . . didn't know . . .' his voice trailed off.

She laughed at him, a shy, tender sound. '*You*, you with your lessons in love? I thought you knew everything.'

'Almost everything,' he corrected her, his eyes sparkling as he stroked the curve of her breast. 'I assumed that when I found you breakfasting with Adam, he'd finished the lesson.'

Clarissa gazed at him in astonishment and he shrugged, looking rueful, while his eyes loved her.

He rose to pour them both some champagne and beneath half closed lids she watched the powerful male body so recently, so mysteriously entwined with hers, and marvelled at its lean straight lines, the strong thighs, the taut stomach and broad, muscled shoulders. Suddenly she remembered the ceiling of the Sistine Chapel where she had stood in mute misery, trying desperately not to think of Garrett. The laughter bubbled in her and he bent over her to nip her lips with a light kiss. 'Now be a good girl and stop laughing at my fragile male ego,' he teased her.

Her eyes shone over him and shyly she touched him, fingering the rough, dark hair on his chest as he lay beside her, one arm propped behind his head, his eyes sultry beneath the half-closed lids. Still shyly she explored the texture of his skin, her fingers now so acutely sensitive that the touch sent ripples of sensation through her. He pulled her to him, entwining his long legs with hers and kissed her with a lingering tenderness, an intensity so sweet that again she could feel her limbs turning molten, the blood beginning to pound in her. Garrett's hands, his lips, his breath stroked, caressed, intoxicated her, so that when he entered her again, slowly, gently, tantalisingly, flexing his body against hers, moulding her to him, Clarissa knew that the waves of feeling flooding through her could only bear his name. She spoke it hoarsely again and again as her body called to him, stirred for him, and she met the consuming fire of his eyes for an infinite moment as their mingled passion delivered them to a timeless region where they existed purely as themselves and yet each other.

They lay clasped in each other's arms, their eyes murmuring until sleep overtook them and when Clarissa woke the next morning to a shy light, a hum played over her lips. She stretched blissfully, not yet fully aware of her surroundings, and as memory returned, she lazily put out a hand towards Garrett's warmth, only to find an empty space which bore the indentation of his body. A fear rose in her blood, but then he was at her side, his eyes flickering over her face, his hands stroking hers. He was dressed, dark trousers hugging his muscular thighs, a pale striped shirt casually clothing his frame. Deep inside her something stirred again and her arms rose of their own accord to embrace him. His smile played with her.

'Breakfast in bed on this very special day, Madame Harlowe? I had some sent up when I went to see to the children. I didn't want Ted scampering into this den of iniquity.'

Clarissa propped herself up on the pillows and made a great show of drawing the sheet up to her chin.

'That's right,' drawled Garrett, 'keep yourself well covered or I may find myself succumbing to temptation!' Through the sheets, his eyes traced the line of her body and suddenly his expression changed and he looked at her with an urgent seriousness.

'Are you all right, Clarissa?' he asked in a low voice. 'Was it,' he paused eyeing her intently, 'was it all right? Did I hurt you?'

She looked at him balefully for a moment and nodded, then as she saw a frown begin to furrow his brow, she flung her arms around him in so ardent a gesture that she almost upset the tray he had placed on the bed. 'It was wonderful,' she whispered in his ear. 'Wonderful—you know it was.' She met his eyes for a long moment and then added wickedly, 'You can give me lessons in love any time!'

The sheet had strayed from her bosom and he fondled her reflectively, 'I don't think you need too many more, my little wild cat,' he murmured. His eyes bright, he kissed her lightly on the lips and again Clarissa felt her body stir to his merest touch. He moved away, fetching his coffee. 'Behave,' he ordered with mock severity. 'We're meant to be responsible adults.'

She reached for her coffee and on the tray she noticed a small box, delicately wrapped in silver paper. She looked at Garrett questioningly.

'For you,' he smiled.

She opened it, her fingers trembling. Inside there was a necklace of beautifully wrought flowers of Venetian glass—the finest amber, the palest greens catching the light's reflection. 'It's beautiful,' she breathed, marvelling at the craft which had caught nature and held it in a perfect moment. Garrett fixed it round her neck, caressing her lightly.

They bantered over their coffee and made plans for the day. Then Clarissa gathered a sheet round her nakedness and went to bathe and dress. In the large bathroom mirror with its ornate oval frame, she gazed at the body which no longer seemed altogether hers and wondered whether it showed the traces of what she felt.

Her head seemed to be ringing with a hundred clichés which in another state, or sitting at her typewriter, she would have snorted at. She laughed at herself. She did indeed feel she was walking on air, riding on a cloud, a new buoyancy in her gestures, a strangely provocative smile set on her wide lips, the honey-gold flecks in her blue eyes suddenly brighter.

Silly, she scoffed at herself, and deliberately tugged on habitual clothes, a pair of snug jeans, a soft, much laundered woolly jumper, and went to meet the day. Garrett was waiting for her with Ted and Elinor in the lobby. A secret look passed between them as she walked towards him, and it was only with difficulty that she could keep her fingers from rising to touch his strong face.

Much as he tried to persuade her that they could, if she wished, go off on their own, Clarissa insisted that they should all stay together. Garrett smiled at her warmly, pleased, she thought, at her insistence, and the day unfolded with that miraculousness the city seemed to have as its own particular property. The four of them piled into gondolas or *motoscaffi*—Ted's preferred mode of transport; walked through countless *piazzetti*, one more wondrous than the next; roamed across a near deserted Lido which seemed to be caught in a nineteenth-century stillness; watched lustrous glass being formed; gazed at mosaics of the clearest blue.

At one point when Elinor and Clarissa were walking together, the younger girl said, 'I'm so pleased you and Garrett are happy together.'

Clarissa coloured and Elinor's dark, knowing eyes flashed. 'You almost deserve him,' she chuckled, and then with her customary expansiveness, she kissed Clarissa's cheek and winked.

'Time for some more ice cream, ladies,' Garrett urged them on, and they laughed, having already consumed more than any person over the age of six could bear. Over the laughter, Garrett and Clarissa exchanged a secret look, charged with warmth, memory and a rising anticipation.

At the end of a packed day, when Ted had been securely tucked in for the evening and Clarissa had finished the second instalment of her Venetian saga, he looked mischievously at her and Garrett. 'Only nine hundred and ninety-nine nights left to go, right, Dad?'

Garrett groaned, 'I don't think either Clarissa or I could manage that!'

Clarissa glanced at him, a shudder suddenly running through her. How many nights did Garrett think they *could* manage together?

'Yes, you could. You're almost as good as Laura,' Ted insisted, and then looked at Clarissa with a child's inperiousness. 'And don't forget I'm counting!'

Clarissa tried a smile and kissed the little boy goodnight. She didn't like the analogy with his dead mother, but it was Garrett's comment which lingered in her, upset her, and as she walked to her room, she worked to bury it at the farthest recesses of her mind. No sooner had she closed her door behind her than a knock announced him. He walked in smiling and swept her into his arms, lifting her off her feet to meet his lips. 'I've been waiting to do that all day,' he murmured, nuzzling her ear, before kissing her again, softly, urgently so that her heart set up a wild pounding and the waves started to lap at her stomach.

Then he stepped back and holding her at arm's length gazed at her. Clarissa realised that only in the rare moments when she had seen him playing with Ted had the discordant features of his dramatic face looked so at one as they had throughout this long day. Now his mobile lips curved into a wide smile and the blue-black of his eyes sparkled. 'We're going to be grand this evening and dine in the hotel. I've got some phone calls to make, so you can take your time getting dressed.' He gave her a slow languorous wink. 'Come and fetch me when you're ready.'

But Clarissa was ready far before the appointed time. She realised she didn't want to be alone, didn't want her mind to set to work, and with a grimace of hesitation, she went to knock at his door.

'Come in,' his voice beckoned her, and she opened the door to find him standing by the telephone. He was wearing a deep blue towelling robe which emphasised the breadth of his shoulders, and seeing him standing their nonchalantly speaking into the instrument while his eyes trailed over her, Clarissa suddenly felt an intruder and made to leave. Garrett gestured her in, pointing to an open wine bottle on the window table, and she settled into a chair nearby, trying not to overhear his conversation.

When he had finished, he turned to her with gleaming eyes. 'Your book is doing well,' a grin spread over his face. 'Are you pleased that I'm going to win my bet?'

'Decidedly.' Her eyes flashed at him. 'As long as I don't have Bianca's marketing talents to thank for it.'

'Miaow!' he purred at her, then he gathered together some clothes and was off into the bathroom.

Clarissa looked randomly round the room and then went to stand by the window to gaze at the lights flickering in the lagoon. An ache of uncertainty seemed to be gnawing at her entrails. There was only one thing she knew for certain: she loved Garrett, loved him as she had never loved anyone before, as she had never imagined love could envelop her or even exist. But everything else was opaque. She didn't understand how he could make excuses for Bianca. She still didn't know whether he felt anything more for her than a passing desire, which conveniently also seemed to suit his son. It suddenly occurred to her that he had never taken her to his flat in Manhattan. Perhaps her presence there wouldn't be tolerable. Perhaps the memory of his wife, or even Bianca, presided over that territory to the exclusion of anyone else. Clarissa shrugged. Garrett's experience of life was so much vaster than hers. Intellectually she knew that passion—which she sensed he felt for her—did not necessarily equal love, certainly not its continuity. She also knew that she had always thought it would be immoral to barter her own passion, her love, for marriage. That was why, she guessed, it hadn't occurred to her to ask anything of Garrett last night, to hold back because he had made no promises. But she knew she yearned for some kind of affirmation of continuity, some extension of their passion into real time.

She didn't hear him emerge until he was beside her and his arms which encircled her from behind, startled her.

'Pensive, little one? Staring out of windows is meant to be a dangerous pastime in Venice.'

She turned in the circle of his arms and looked deeply, seriously into his eyes. He held her at arm's length and examined her face. His eyes grew troubled. 'Are you having second thoughts, Clarissa?'

She shrugged. 'Third and fourth thoughts.'

He drew her closely to him and kissed her eyes, the curve of her cheek, and lightly pressed her lips. She nuzzled against him, breathing in the clean male smell of him. 'My love,' he murmured against her hair, 'my love!' She thrilled to his words and pressed more closely against him. 'We're exhausting you, aren't we? I keep forgetting what a fraught time it's been.'

Clarissa shook her head and looked up at him radiantly.

'I'm just hungry.'

He groaned, but his eyes were still serious, examining her. 'That at least can be instantly remedied.'

They went down to the restaurant arm in arm and sat at a table overlooking the Grand Canal. Clarissa felt once again that they had created a space around them, which like the city itself, existed out of time. She savoured each moment, each look that passed between them, each morsel of food, each word, as if it were an entity somehow raised beyond them, like the resonant phrases of a poem; or, she thought with a pang which seemed to cut her almost in two, as if it would disappear all too quickly and needed to be stored in a cherished memory.

Unconsciously she registered each of Garrett's expressions, the flux of his features as he talked, for this evening he did talk about himself: the childhood which seemed to exist for him as an idyll ruptured by his mother's death. At one moment, the tale he told evoked such poignancy for her—though his words were crisply unsentimental and full of self-irony—that the tears gathered at the backs of her eyes and she reached for his hand.

He skirted the subject of his wife, yet when she did skirmish into their conversation, his gaze turned black and the intentness with which he looked at Clarissa gave her a strange sensation: as if the woman were vibrantly alive, standing beside her now, her long hair curling—and Clarissa felt she was being judged in her image. She shuddered, blocking out the sensation, leaving the painful subject of her own accord. She wished she had been bold enough to ask Elizabeth about Garrett's past. Yet when with a mute gesture he kissed her fingertips, she forgot everything but the sheer call of his tangible presence, which mesmerised her, bound her to him irrevocably.

Their lovemaking that night took on a depth, an intensity that seemed to penetrate her most secret core and reveal it to her anew. Her flesh quickened to his passion, aroused a sensitivity of response at once violent and gentle so that she learned a language of touch whose richness her wildest dreams had never suspected—senses signalling the most subtle and varied nuances of feeling. And at last, when a deep, sweet shuddering convulsed his body, it mirrored her own uncontrollable trembling. A peace mingled with tears descended on her and she slept, her body as entwined with his as her dreams.

She woke to find herself still coiled in his embrace, and for a moment, before his eyes opened in response to hers, she took in the rugged yet strangely vulnerable beauty of his features. A sense of wonder filled her, mixed with fear at the fragility of the moment. Garrett held her closely to him and kissed her with a warmth born of knowledge. A quivering rose in them both, yet Clarissa shook herself mentally and drew away. 'It's my turn to see to Ted,' she whispered to him. 'You sleep in.'

He protested. 'He's perfectly all right. I told Elinor to take him down for breakfast.'

Clarissa glanced at her watch and groaned comically. 'Breakfast is about to turn into lunch at any moment!' With a swift movement, she gathered up her tumbled clothes. 'Rest, that's an order.'

'Yes, madame.' He looked at her humorously, affectionately, and she bent to kiss him lightly before turning away.

Clarissa showered and quickly put on trousers and a fresh jumper. One look out of her window told her that the weather had changed dramatically. Beneath a steel-grey sky the waters of the canal lashed against buildings, and swirled on to the pavement of the square. She shuddered, pulled her coat out of the closet and made her way downstairs.

She found Elinor reading a picture book to Ted, who was bursting to go outdoors and play in the puddles. Clarissa offered to take him out and the child smiled at her gleefully.

'You're much nicer than the stepmothers in the fairy tales, Clarissa,' he told her as they walked through the lobby.

She ruffled the small boy's hair. 'Maybe that's because I'm not your stepmother.'

'Oh, but you will be,' he asserted evenly. 'I've told Dad that I want you to be.'

Clarissa swallowed hard. 'And what did he say?' she asked, keeping her voice light.

Ted shrugged as if he were much older than his years. 'Oh, he's always a bit slow in making up his mind. But he'll come round. And then,' he looked at her excitedly, 'you can tell me stories every night!'

'Yes,' Clarissa murmured, fear aching through her.

When Ted had satisfied his desire for puddles, they returned to the hotel and leaving the child in Elinor's capable hands, Clarissa went in search of Garrett. He wasn't in his room, and as she looked for him, Clarissa wondered rather guiltily whether her affection for and patience with Ted might not in part be a ploy for reaching his father's heart. She handled the thought, examined it with an attempt at cold lucidity, though it was difficult for her now to separate out her feelings for the tall man and the small boy. Yet she remembered distinctly how much she had liked Ted before even realising he was his father's son.

On an offchance, she wandered into a small dimly-lit bar she had never entered before and looked round for Garrett. Suddenly she rubbed her eyes, as if to wipe away a bad dream. Sitting at a low table were Bianca and Garrett, deep in conversation, their eyes intent on one another. Bianca's hand rose to Garrett's shoulder. It wasn't possible! Clarissa's breath caught in her throat.

She felt confusion cloud her vision and turned quickly on her heel before they could spot her. In a daze she walked through the lobby. How could he? How could he? Her mind reeled. How could he look like that into the woman's eyes, be with her—the woman who had plotted against her, whom he had said he didn't love; a woman whom any sensible man would have had reported, fired, anything but this! Clarissa lurched along, the blood thudding through her temples, a dizziness rising through her. He had lied to her.

As she approached the reception desk, she heard a voice distinctly asking for Garrett Hamilton. She paused and took in the speaker: a wonderfully attractive woman with softly waving dark hair. In the next instant, responding to the receptionist's query, the woman identified herself. Clarissa's heart seemed to stop dead. Laura Hamilton, she had heard the woman enunciate precisely

Aghast, Clarissa drew away and watched the woman from a safe distance.

He had said his wife was dead.

As the photographs she had seen of Garrett's wife flashed through her head with accelerating swiftness, juxtaposed with moments Clarissa had lived with him, she felt she was drowning, struggling for breath. She sank into a nearby armchair and watched, as if her life depended on the accuracy of her vision. The woman paced in front of the reception desk, the skirt of her elegant grey suit swishing over her shapely stockinged legs. Then Clarissa saw Ted emerge from nowhere and hurl himself into the woman's arms. She hugged him and listened to his excited babble.

With her remaining ounce of strength, she huddled into her coat and walked swiftly, silently, out of the hotel.

CHAPTER NINE

A BITTER wind whipped at Clarissa's cheeks as she crossed the square. She tasted salt on her lips, unsure whether it was the flavour of the moist sea wind or her own tears. Water swirled round her feet and without knowing in which direction she was heading, she went into St Mark's, as if its glistening, timeless interior might protect her from her own inner storm as well as the one which had so rampantly invaded the city.

But the church smelled dank; its chill air exuded a sense of decay. Blindly, Clarissa walked. First Bianca, then his wife. Her shoes on the cold floor tapped out the rhythm of the names with an insistent clack. Garrett had woven a tissue of lies for her consumption. And dupe that she was, she had believed him. Now his past had suddenly stormed in on them, engulfed them, shattering the fragility of their moment, their Venetian fairytale. She had been a fool to believe that it wouldn't; that history wouldn't erupt into the time-stopped magic of their togetherness and break it asunder. She remembered some don years ago, trying to make her understand that without a sense of the past there was no possibility of a future. And Garrett had deliberately omitted the significant past and conjured up no sense of a united future. All they had was a moment of magic, a present heightened out of time. Perhaps it was enough, Clarissa tried to convince herself through her tears: like an ikon one returned to in memory but which played no part in the continuity of one's life.

Suddenly she knew exactly what she must do. Like some fugitive whose first principles are speed and anonymity, she hurried back to the hotel, stealthily crossed the lobby and made her way to her room where, within minutes, she had packed her few belongings. At the door, she paused and turning back, took some notepaper from the writing table and penned two quick messages. To Garrett she wrote with a sure knowledge of the painful ironies, 'Thanks for the lesson in love'; and to Ted and Elinor, a longer note, wishing them a happy stay, saying they must come to see her in England if their travels ever took them there.

As the lift door opened on to the lobby, Clarissa looked round carefully and then went over to leave her envelopes at the reception desk. Luck was with her, she thought with only a hint of bitterness. None of them were in sight. As if she had already been forgotten. But she mustn't let herself sink into self-pity.

She had just reached the hotel door when she heard her name from behind her. Her instant reaction was to flee, to pretend she hadn't heard, but an arm dropped on her shoulder and she turned to see Marco Fiorucci.

'I was hoping you would turn up. They told me at the desk you were still here.' He took in the small suitcase she was holding. 'You're not leaving already?'

Clarissa nodded. 'I've got to get back to England. I'm just off to the airport.'

'And Garrett?' His dark eyes quizzed her.

'He's with his family.' Clarissa kept her voice as cool as she could, though the words seemed to choke her. 'I didn't want to drag them all the way to the airport.'

'Perhaps we still have time for a quick drink together?'

She glanced at her watch as if she had a distinct idea of plane schedules, and shook her head.

'Well then, I shall accompany you. It would be sad if there was no one to see you off from our country.' Marco took her bag from her.

Not wanting to stand there talking any longer, Clarissa accepted his offer. She looked a little furtively round the large room and her legs grew weak. She could see Garrett at the other end of the lobby. With an effort which seemed to drain her totally, she preceded Marco swiftly through the door. The hotel boat was at its mooring, and breathing a sigh of relief, she stepped into it, while Marco explained their destination.

As they sped through the canal, Clarissa cast a last look at the city. Even in the grey wintry light, it looked like some grand monument—a monument to my love, she thought, trying to keep the tears from flooding down her face.

When she arrived in London, it was already dark, and although she knew that she should feel she had managed a brilliant escape—the fact that they weren't hours too early for a plane had saved her some embarrassment with Marco—she felt, in fact, abysmally lost. Heathrow seemed to have spawned innumerable new additions, and the sound of her native English rang oddly in her ears.

Her plans had only taken her as far as flight, and now, her small suitcase in her hand, she didn't quite know where to turn. She decided it would be best to ring her brother and see if he could put her up for one night at least. She had long ago given up her London bedsit. Luck was on her side, she thought with a glimmer of irony. Michael was still in his office, and though he registered some surprise at her unannounced arrival, he asked no questions, simply telling her to climb into a taxi. They would probably reach his flat at about the same time.

With the sense of a sleepwalker, Clarissa drove through a sprawling London, its sheer expanse, the randomness of its structure unfamiliar after the compactness of Manhattan's grid. As the taxi passed through Little Venice, Clarissa shivered. What she needed least now were reminders. She knew it was only the necessity of instant action which had kept her from crumbling totally in the last few hours.

Michael was already back in his Maida Vale flat when she arrived, and he hugged her warmly as she walked through the door.

'What deities do I have to thank for this surprise visit?' he teased her, and then taking in the look on her face stopped and gazed at her in concern. He ushered her into the sitting-room, fetched a bottle of brandy and gesturing her towards a chair sat down opposite her. 'What's up, Clarissa? This is not the cheerful, successful young woman I met at Frankfurt so very short a time ago.'

She shrugged and tried to meet his tone. 'I'm still relatively successful. It's only the smile that's vanished.'

'Temporarily, I hope, little sister.'

Clarissa sipped the burning liquid and looked into the eyes which were so like hers.

'I hope so too.'

'Are you going to tell me about him?'

'Him?'

'Oh, don't look so innocent, Clary,' Michael cuffed her playfully. 'I wasn't born yesterday.'

'I don't think I can talk about it just yet,' she murmured.

Michael sipped his brandy reflectively. 'Any plans?'

She shrugged. 'I thought I'd go down to the Tower and stay there for a while.'

'We'll go down together if you like. Tomorrow's Saturday and I haven't seen the young ones for a while.'

Clarissa smiled at the familiar ephithet they used for their parents, and suddenly the tears streamed from her eyes. Michael put his arm round her comfortingly and she let herself cry into his shoulder, give vent to a misery which seemed boundless and inconsolable.

On the drive down to Sussex, Clarissa sketched the broad outlines of her relationship with Garrett in response to Michael's probing questions.

'But, Clary,' he protested, 'all this running away is nonsense. You don't know why he's seeing Bianca—it might be business. You don't know whether he cares a hoot for his wife, don't even know whether she's his *ex*-wife or not?'

Clarissa had to admit that this was true. But then she hadn't told Michael everything; hadn't told him about the burglary, about the way in which she had been led to believe, or simply wanted to believe, that Garrett's wife was dead. She couldn't put into words her acute sense of betrayal at what seemed to be Garrett's toying with her, his deliberate omissions of fact, omissions which became, in retrospect, tantamount to lies. To Michael, she simply said, 'But the child—he was so pleased to see her. I couldn't intrude on that.'

He looked at her astutely. 'Are you sure you're not exaggerating that, simply feeling guilty for having usurped the mother's role?'

Clarissa looked at him blankly and her brother shrugged, 'Let's drop it for now.'

They had turned into the dirt road which led them up to the Tower and she opened her window and put her head through it to breathe in the moist country air which smelled at once of grass and clay, sharpened by the salt tang of the sea. Her early childhood appeared before her in a flash, and with a mute sigh she wished that things were as simple now as they had been then, when any companion other than her brother had seemed an encumbrance.

The familiar grey slabs of the Martello tower, perched on its gentle slope, came into view, and once again Clarissa was struck by its fairytale quality. It was no wonder that her sense of reality was somewhat dim—she scoffed at herself—if this turret, this misty countryside with its muted greens and greys, had shaped her inner landscape.

Her mother and father came through the door just as Michael switched off the ignition, and Clarissa hurried up the remainder of the hill to greet them. She noticed both how they had aged and how clear their eyes were. As she embraced them, she realised, too, how the years had made them increasingly like one another, eradicated, by the growing similarity of expression and gesture, many of the differences in size and shape. She was suddenly aware, too, that it was her parents' very contentment with one another that had occasionally made her feel an outsider in their company. Perhaps that was why—the idea hit her with a thud—she had been so attracted by Ted, by Garrett. They had seemed to need her. But now . . . She forced herself to focus on her parents.

They welcomed her warmly, as if she were some returning heroine who had survived innumerable battles.

'A bit peaked,' her father examined her. 'You could do with some walks and some of your mother's food. Which shall it be first?'

'A walk,' Michael and Clarissa said in unison, and laughed at their instantaneous reaction.

'You go ahead,' their mother beamed at them. 'I'll put some lunch on the table.'

Pulling on the familiar wellies which seemed to have been perched in the same spot for years, Michael and Clarissa grinned at each other.

'Things don't change much around here,' he said to her.

'We should be grateful,' she countered him.

The three of them trekked over the downs in the soft wintry drizzle, their progress slowed by the gathering mud on their boots. Clarissa cherished each remembered vista as it unfolded before her, trying as best she could in the monumental peace of these ancient hills to forget the many changes which had taken place in her. The pheasants scattered at their passing and in the distance she could hear the faint sound of gunshots.

'They're at it again,' her father said disapprovingly. 'It seems to get worse each year—more and more of them shooting.'

Clarissa put a hand on his shoulder. 'Done any good pictures lately, Dad?'

He chuckled. 'You still remember how to turn my mind away from anything else! I'll show you when we get back.'

Clarissa's room was exactly as she had left it, one rounded side overlooking the gently rolling hills; the other forming a corner with Michael's room. She changed into an old pair of jeans and a thick woolly jumper for lunch. In the kitchen which occupied the entire ground floor of the Tower, they ate her mother's thick soup and roast lamb round a long refectory table, while Clarissa was forced to recount her adventures in New York, then Frankfurt and Rome. She omitted Venice, knowing that her voice which had already grown to an unnatural pitch of exuberance would crack under the strain. As it was, the narration had taken far too long, and by the time they were sipping their coffee in front of the blazing fire in the sitting room upstairs, the early winter night had already descended.

Michael glanced at his watch. 'I'm going to have to head back to London.'

'You're not!' Clarissa looked at him in astonishment. 'Aren't you staying the night?'

Michael shook his head, while their mother laughed. 'He's got to get back to his girl, haven't you, Michael?'

Michael nodded a little sheepishly, while Clarissa looked at him in amazement. He hadn't said anything to her. But then she guessed she hadn't given him much of a chance. A twinge of fear gripped her stomach at the thought of her encroaching isolation, just, she remembered, as it had done when Michael's school holidays were over and he had been set to leave the Tower. She shook herself mentally, ashamed at her own childishness. Yet she knew that with Michael away, she would be forced back on herself as her parents' lives followed their own slow course.

'She's very nice, Clary,' Michael's voice startled her out of herself. 'You'll meet her when you're next in London. Or we'll both come down next weekend.'

'That would be super,' she said, hoping that her tremulousness didn't show.

Clarissa's life settled into an uneasy rhythm which she knew couldn't last, but which she didn't have the energy or the will to break. She realised that she should arrange to go back to New York and collect her belongings, settle things about the loft, the cats. But she couldn't bring herself to make plans. She just managed to write to Elizabeth to say that she was taking a break with her parents. Did she need her fur coat back?

Elizabeth replied that she needn't worry, that she looked forward to having her back in New York soon, that the book was doing well. And that, as far as Clarissa was concerned, was the end of her contact with New York. No word came from Garrett, though she imagined that Elizabeth must have told him where she was. It confirmed her in the fact that her flight had been right, that at least there had been no verbal squabbles to blight their perfect Venetian memory. The bitterness welled up in her. Over the weeks it turned into a permanent ache, just barely containable by day, but which festered painfully in the darkness of night.

A recurrent dream plagued her into sleeplessness. She was driving along in the Lancia with Garrett, Ted and Elinor; the headlights and then the impact came and with a piercing clarity she knew she was dead, though her body on the gleaming white of the stretcher could see the others distinctly as they walked away from her, holding hands.

She tried, for her parents' sake, to act naturally. She accompanied her father on walks, went into the neighbouring town with her mother to do the shopping. On one of these occasions she bought an old, beautifully bound copy of T. S. Eliot's *Practical Cats* and sent it off with a little note to Ted.

She met Michael's girl-friend, a pretty fellow publisher, and was amazed to find herself jealous of what seemed their evident happiness. She scolded herself and went out of her way to be charming to the girl, and tell Michael how lovely she was.

'Things will sort themselves out for you too,' he replied, hugging her.

The tears came to Clarissa's eyes. It hardly seemed likely, she thought, when her nights were spent in an agony of longing and her days in a barely contained grief, which smacked of nothing so much as mourning. She spent hours sitting at her desk trying to write. But her new novel seemed to have died in her, desperately as she wanted to revive it. If she somehow managed to complete a page, it would immediately find its way into the dustbin. Most of the time, her mind was trammelled by memories of Garrett, instants so vivid, so charged with their aftermath of pain, that she lost all track of the present until her mother's voice would startle her back into its reality.

In an effort to break the pattern, she began to accompany her mother to her little workshop. She had learned to throw pots at a young age, and now the sense of clay taking shape in her hands gave her momentary relief. During one of these sessions, her mother paused in her own work and looked at her closely.

'I know we've never been much for confessionals in this family, Clarissa. But it might help if we talked. You seem to grow more miserable every day.'

'I'm having trouble with my writing,' Clarissa tried to brush her comment aside. 'It'll pass.'

Her mother looked at her with an astuteness Clarissa didn't recollect in her. 'Are you sure that's what it is, Clarissa? I thought there might be something more.'

Clarissa shrugged and her mother turned to her work for a few moments, stacking pitchers of various sizes on shelves.

Then she sat down at Clarissa's side. 'I never told you about your father and me, Clarissa, did I? You always seemed too young, such a child.' A light twinkled in her mother's eye. 'You know, he left me once, at the very beginning of things. I thought, literally thought I would die. Nothing seemed worth doing any more.'

Clarissa looked at her mother strangely, at the pain which seemed to have darkened her features.

Her mother smiled, as she read her expression on her daughter's face. 'Well, then, after some months of this living death, he wrote to me to say,' she suddenly laughed out loud, 'that he had gone away because he didn't think such emotion could last, that it was better to have a perfect moment fixed for ever in memory, than the terrible attenuation of it all in the squalid routine of everyday life.'

'Go on,' Clarissa urged as her mother paused.

'Well, I thought about this for a while, as well as I

could, because I still felt more dead than alive, and then, after having initially agreed with him, I grew angry, so angry that I caught the next train and went to the address he'd given on his letter.' Her face lit up and Clarissa could see exactly how she must have looked as a young woman.

'I screamed at him, called him, among other less noble things, a perfidious romantic, a coward who was afraid of life, and then I stormed away. He came after me a few days later.'

'But that's not at all like me,' Clarissa breathed.

'I know,' her mother chuckled. 'I just thought you might like to exchange confidences.'

'All right, you win,' Clarissa groaned, giving her mother a rare squeeze. And then she told her at least a little about Garrett.

'I see,' her mother said, looking at her carefully. 'It is rather complicated.' She offered no advice, only asking, 'But you are planning to go back to New York.'

Clarissa shrugged. 'I'll have to at some point to clear out the flat.'

That night she sat at her little writing desk leafing through Shakespeare's Sonnets, while at the back of her mind, her mother's story played itself out. A line leapt off the page at her:

A liquid prisoner pent in walls of glass.

Suddenly, every moment of her days in Venice with Garrett seemed to crystallise into a single image which rent her in two. She wrote the line on a sheet of paper, gazing at it, meditating on its many senses, and with a wry, dawning self-awareness, she realised that she was distinctly her father's daughter, a perfidious romantic. With a burst of energy she began to sketch a story in which the characters, lightly veiled were herself and Garrett, caught in a beautiful time-stopped bubble of love which simultaneously shielded and imprisoned them. She worked until late in the night and for the first time in weeks, she fell asleep without the tears streaming into her pillow.

But by the next morning, the story seemed to have receded into a zone which wouldn't, however tortured, find expression in words, and in a rage she flung herself on her bed, letting the sobs rack her until she was utterly exhausted. Dizzily she picked herself off the bed and went to splash cold water on her swollen features. Her face in the mirror looked back at her strangely. Do something with yourself, it ordered. And she knew that very soon she would have to. Christmas was almost upon them, and after that she could find no excuse for trailing on in her parents' house, let alone the fact that she would have to go back to New York and sort out the matter of the flat.

'Letter for you, Clarissa!' her mother's voice wove its way up the circular staircase. Clarissa went down the stairs and picked up the airmail envelope with shaking hands. The writing was unfamiliar and when she tore it open, she found a thank you from Ted, a picture of a sad cat. Under it he had printed in large, slightly shaky letters, 'Miss you'.

'Good news?' her mother questioned her.

Clarissa passed her the picture and sighed. The son, if not the father, missed her, which was somehow appropriate since the whole thing had really begun with Ted.

Pulling on an old mac, Clarissa went out for a walk, only to return to find her mother in a strangely excited state.

'Your American publisher's here!'

Clarissa clutched at the back of a chair, her legs reeling under her.

'She asked if she could come down here for the day tomorrow.'

'She?' Clarissa queried, the colour draining from her face.

'Yes, Elizabeth something. She said she was dying to see you, dying to see this place and she had the proofs of your new book—which I,' her mother added wryly, 'am dying to read.'

'I see,' Clarissa said listlessly.

'Come on,' her mother bullied her. 'We have to move, get some food in, clean this place. She's arriving on the eleven o'clock train and I said we'd meet her at the station.'

Clarissa complied, helping her mother to Hoover and scrub as if royalty were expected; getting in groceries, rolling out pastry. At least, she thought as all the unexpected activity worked on her nerve ends, Elizabeth's arrival provided a change.

'Why, this is exquisite!' Elizabeth's merry blue eyes grew wide in her face as she took in the spectacle of the Martello tower. 'No wonder you write so well about the country!'

Clarissa smiled. The old Austin Morris had just ground to a halt in the thick Sussex mud, its wheels spinning fruitlessly. 'But I keep forgetting to mention the mud. Here,' she handed Elizabeth a pair of wellies from under the car's seat. 'I hope they fit, or your elegant New York boots will never look the same.'

Elizabeth trudged up the hill between Clarissa and her mother. At every step she exclaimed her delight with what she saw before her. 'I'm so pleased you invited me down, Mrs Harlowe.'

Clarissa looked at her mother questioningly, but she gazed innocently away from her, replying to Elizabeth, 'I thought you might enjoy it.'

And with the bubbling enthusiasm which Clarissa had all but forgotten, Elizabeth did indeed seem to enjoy it. She insisted on examining every part of the Tower, handling each of her mother's pots and surveying all of her father's watercolours. It seemed too that she was intent on taking at least a third of it all home with her. 'You didn't know I was a compulsive collector,' she murmured to Clarissa, when her mother said they could talk about all that after lunch.

Lunch passed in a flurry of conversation, and Clarissa watched with a degree of surprise how well her parents and Elizabeth seemed to get on. She flushed as the woman recounted her New York successes, while her mother shook her head, saying that Clarissa had never told them about any of this. When it was time for coffee, Clarissa found herself being authoritatively sent upstairs with Elizabeth, so that they could have a quiet chat, her mother explained.

With a degree of hesitation, Clarissa acquiesced. She didn't quite know what to say to Elizabeth and the shrewd eyes which examined her would brook no evasions.

'You look dreadful,' were Elizabeth's first words after Mrs Harlowe had closed the door behind her.

Clarissa shrugged and tried a smile. 'This is how I always look around here. There's not much point in dressing up.'

Elizabeth took no note of her words. 'Almost as bad as Garrett!' The older woman eyed her astutely as Clarissa's brows shot up. 'What's with the two of you? He comes back from Europe without you and in a rage which never seems to abate. Either he's shrieking at everybody or sitting at his desk, lost in Never-Never-Land. He doesn't tell me why you've decided to go back to England. I come here and find you looking like a scarecrow who's just survived some British variation of the Gulag. What's up?'

Clarissa's smile at Elizabeth's description vanished as soon as she felt her eyes on her.

'Come on, hon. The two of you are mad for each other—that's been clear to me from the beginning. Own up and tell me what's gone wrong.'

Clarissa met Elizabeth's inspection with a grimace.

'He's married, Elizabeth. And I'm just not made like that.'

Elizabeth looked at her strangely. 'You've gone raving mad, Clarissa! Garrett's wife died about three years ago.'

Astonishment spread over Clarissa's features and she got up from her chair, unable to sit still, and stood gazing incomprehendingly out the window.

'And Laura—Laura Hamilton? Who is she?' Clarissa turned to look at Elizabeth.

'Hasn't the man told you anything? Damn his secrecy! She's his sister—his stepsister.'

Clarissa's mouth flew open. 'I'm a fool,' she groaned. 'An even bigger fool than I thought!'

'I don't know what's the matter with you young people any more. Don't you talk to each other? And the two of you are meant to be literate!' Elizabeth scolded her, holding her hands out in front of her with a gesture of exasperation.

Suddenly a shrill laugh rose in Clarissa's throat. Through it, she pleaded, 'I kept trying to ask him, but he avoided the subject any time I came close.'

Elizabeth shook her head and sighed, half in impatience, half in concern. 'I guess it's still a painful subject for him. Right, Clarissa, here goes, for your illumination.

'Garret was married to one of our rich young belles, Dahlia Barker. She was something of a spoiled brat, a wealthy man's only daughter, and I think she decided she would have him. Garrett, even then, was worth having. They had a fling, I guess, and a few months later she arrives, announcing that she's pregnant. Garrett, to his credit, does the right thing. She was very young, very beautiful, and I think he was half in love with her already. In any case, when I first met them together he was passionate about her, so perhaps he would have married her, pregnancy or no pregnancy.'

Clarissa felt a lump of jealousy rise in her throat.

'Well, then Ted is born, and a few months later, Dahlia ups and leaves them, wanders off with another man, some idiot of a Californian. No excuses, simply that she's bored with being a mother.'

'I don't believe it!' Clarissa gasped. 'Garrett must have mistreated her.'

'Well, do believe it. If anything Garrett errs on the side of kindness. In any case, I have it not from Garrett, but from an aunt of hers, who's an old friend. And Dahlia herself had no qualms about talking. Life, as far as she was concerned, had to be exciting; and being stuck with a baby—despite all the help she could

possibly want—wasn't much fun for her. The
Californian was.

'Well, then Garrett takes a leave of absence from
work—does editing part-time from home—and for the
next few months devotes himself to the child. Lunacy!
Until the vagrant Dahlia turns up again and decides
she's going to be a good mum after all, as well as find a
job. The Californian got boring. So Garrett takes her
back. He's still in love with her, I think; but perhaps it
was for Ted's sake. Dahlia's father finds her work in an
advertising agency. This lasts for all of six months and
she decides it's no good. The excuse is that she's tired,
she can't cope. The real reason is that there's this other
man. The merry-go-round continues. She comes back
again for a few months and once more she's off, this
time with a French racing car driver.'

Clarissa's eyes widened in disbelief.

'It's true, hon,' Elizabeth laughed. 'I couldn't make
up anything quite so corny. Garrett, from what her
aunt recounts, tells Dahlia that this time it's the end.
Ted is growing up and she can't just pop in and out of
his life for a few months at a time, whenever she fancies
herself in the role of mother. She goes off anyhow, to
France, and the next thing we hear is that there's been
this dreadful car crash. Garrett dashes off to France
somewhere and when he comes back, we learn she's
dead. May she rest in peace, and leave us all some as
well,' Elizabeth finished her narrative.

Clarissa gazed at her, trying to take in this flood of
information, understanding at last the reason behind
the pain which seemed to lurk in Garrett's eyes, his
caution, his suspicion. Her heart turned over. And
here—here she had treated him and Ted in what was
effectively the same way. 'How he must have suffered!'
she breathed at last.

'Hon,' Elizabeth looked at her intently, 'do you love
him?'

Clarissa nodded, feeling the familiar warmth flooding
through her veins as she conjured up his presence. 'Very
much,' she added.

'Well, I may be a meddling old woman and I don't know what's passed between you two. But I do know one thing. If you want him, you're going to have to make it very clear to him. I think I'd have some reservations about women, if I'd been through what he has.'

'But Bianca?' Clarissa asked.

'Bianca!' Elizabeth snorted. 'Bianca Neri has been trying to get Garrett to marry her for years, but he won't. Perhaps because she resents Ted so much, or because the child doesn't really like her. You know how protective he is about that child. I'll give it to Bianca, though, she keeps trying. But now it seems she's going to leave Jethrop House after Christmas.' Elizabeth's eyes twinkled. 'I think you may have had something to do with that, whether you know it or not. She's good at her work, but I think I agree with Ted about her,' she smiled cattily.

'When are you going back to New York, you wicked, meddling old woman?' Clarissa asked suddenly.

'Day after tomorrow.'

'Save me a seat next to yours?'

Elizabeth hugged her, the wrinkles crinkling round her eyes in merriment. 'You bet your life! But you know, Clarissa, you may not have an easy time of it. He's in a really foul temper. Even Ted's not talking back much these days.'

Clarissa shrugged. 'I haven't exactly been feeling on top of the world myself. And as for writing . . . impossible!'

'Which reminds me,' Elizabeth gasped comically, 'I came here to give you your proofs, not to have a hen party,' she gave Clarissa a wicked wink.

'So I believe,' Clarissa smiled at her broadly.

'Well, let's go down and get them then, and I can satisfy my collector's instinct at the same time. Your mother's pots are magnificent!' and Elizabeth was off, chatting away delightedly, while Clarissa could only thank her good fairy that she had woken her from the tortured sleep of the last weeks; and think of Garrett. Garrett, whom—whatever the outcome of her visit—she would see at last.

CHAPTER TEN

As the jumbo jet circled endlessly over Kennedy Airport, Clarissa's mind performed the same motion. Ever since Elizabeth had revealed to her that Garrett's wife was, in fact, dead, and shown her the fool she had been in running away, she had pondered over and over again how best to approach Garrett. It was one thing to explain to him that she had made a mistake on which she had acted in unseemly haste; another to tell him that she loved him. Clarissa swallowed hard. And yet another to prove to him that despite her actions, she was reliable, not a silly, capricious child. Guiltily, she remembered how she had almost killed them all; how she had left Ted, let alone Garrett, without offering any excuse, so that once again the little boy was faced with the mysterious and painful disappearance of a woman who occasionally played mother. How well she understood Garrett's need to protect him, and how little she had contributed to it.

Then too, her mind spun as the plane lurched in an air pocket, Elizabeth didn't seem to know the whole story about Bianca. Bianca, whose unexpected arrival in Venice had sent Clarissa's mind reeling and probably accounted for her unthinking conclusion that Garrett's irrational behaviour included lying about his wife. And even if she accepted Garrett's vagaries concerning Bianca, would Clarissa be brave enough when she was actually faced with him to swallow her pride? In the romances she had always preferred, she admitted to herself sheepishly, the men had won the women over, overwhelmed them with their assiduous wooing, vanquished all seemingly insurmountable obstacles. And here she was placing herself, being placed by circumstance, into the active role: having to face a real man, having to say to him, I want *you*—without being

174

sure, her inner voice reminded her obstinately, that he still wanted her, or indeed had ever wanted her for more than a magical moment of passion.

It's only a slight reversal of roles, she assured herself as the plane finally bumped on to the ground. And what, if anything, have we women been clamouring for all these years but for the freedom not to be locked into a masochistic passivity? She laughed wryly at herself. Funny how difficult it all was when one had to put it to the personal rather than the professional test.

Elizabeth looked at her whimsically. 'Happy to be back?'

'Don't know yet,' Clarissa answered. 'I may not be here for long.'

Elizabeth squeezed her hand. 'Nothing venture . . . I'll tell Garrett you're here first thing in the morning.'

Clarissa's face fell. 'No, don't, Elizabeth. Let me do it in my own time.'

'Well, I don't promise, hon. If he asks me about you, I'll have to say something.'

They shared a taxi back to Manhattan and Elizabeth dropped her at the loft. Clarissa went up the stairs with bated breath. As long as everything was all right here it would be a good sign. She opened the door, which still seemed to be securely locked, looked round and breathed a sigh of relief. Then she went downstairs to see the gallery people who had been looking after the cats in her absence. Given that she had been away much longer than she had said, they seemed not to be terribly upset. They handed her a package which had arrived in the post, and with repeated thanks and a promise to give them a large cheque for cat-food, Clarissa went back upstairs. She opened the package and to her astonishment found the two stolen jade figurines, carefully wrapped. She placed them back on their shelf and sifted through the remaining post.

Bills aside, the only item of interest seemed to be a letter from Adam Bennett asking her to ring him as soon as she was back. Suddenly at a loss as to what to do next, she thought of phoning him immediately, but decided against it. He would ask her about her plans—and her plans, she knew, depended on Garrett. She shivered. Perhaps she should ring *him* now and get it over with. No, she procrastinated, going downstairs again to do some shopping and reacquaint herself with the SoHo streets.

A faint hope had begun to glimmer at the back of her mind, and as soon as it penetrated her consciousness, she scolded herself in disgust. If Elizabeth did tell Garrett she was here, perhaps he would ring her, come to *her*. Despite the scorn she poured on herself, the hope persisted throughout that evening and was still there when she woke in the very early hours of the morning, the jet-lag taking its toll.

Putting off the inevitable and still wishing for the impossible, Clarissa busied herself with cleaning the flat, scrubbing floors, putting a ladder to the windows and scrubbing them, as if somehow she needed to undertake a ritual purification. When there was nothing left to clean, she soaked in the tub until the water grew cold. Then she glanced at her watch. It was already four o'clock.

Cursing her own childish cowardice, she dressed hurriedly and made herself up as she hadn't done for weeks. Beneath the blusher, she noted that her skin looked deadly pale. Perhaps Garrett, beyond anything else, would now find her abysmally unattractive. Clarissa shrugged and forced herself to get on with it, but at the last moment, in order to give herself time to rehearse her scenario once again, she decided to walk to Jethrop House. It'll be almost as quick in the rush hour, she placated her conscience.

A light snow had begun to fall and she idled, relishing the random flakes which dropped before her eyes, stopping to gaze into shop windows. But no matter how much she dallied, she must eventually arrive at Jethrop House. Once within its grand precincts, she threw her shoulders back, passed a hand quickly through her thick hair, slightly moistened by snow, and pushed the lift button for Garrett's floor.

As the lift stopped, she thought with a beating heart, perhaps he's already left, and she didn't know whether she hoped he had or not. Her pulse racing, she pressed the ansaphone buzzer and was asked by Garrett's secretary to wait for a moment while she checked as to whether he would see her without an appointment.

Clarissa waited with bated breath. He was there, but perhaps he wouldn't see her. The secretary's answer seemed to take an inordinately long time. At last her voice came, telling Clarissa to go through.

Hesitantly Clarissa knocked and with the answering 'Come in' opened his door. She stood awkwardly on the threshold, her limbs seeming to give out beneath her as she looked at Garrett standing tall behind his desk. His face looked strained, gaunt, and the blue-black eyes that stared out at her were cold, impatient.

'So it *is* you,' he said brusquely. 'Are you going to come in?'

Clarissa closed the door behind her and willing her legs to carry her forward, she moved towards him, step by step.

'Hello, Garrett,' she murmured, her voice breaking with the effort.

A muscle twitched in his jaw. 'What can I do for you?' he said with cool professionalism.

She slumped into the nearest chair, wishing for once in her life that she smoked, so that she could do something with her restless hands.

'I came to tell you I was back.'

His eyes passed over her coldly, as if she were a lifeless object. 'That's very civil of you.'

'Yes.' She could think of nothing to say, and when he reached for a cigarette, she took one from him, drawing in the acrid taste as if it were the breath of life.

'And how did things go with Marco?' he asked, a bite in his voice.

'Marco?' She looked at him incomprehendingly.

'Yes, you remember,' he spat the words out, his eyes

glacial, 'the man you ditched me for in Venice. Or have there been so many since that you can't remember?'

'Garrett,' his name on her tongue was heavy, 'I didn't . . .' Her voice pleaded with him and suddenly she had to touch him, explain in a language which was so much swifter than words.

But he flinched away from her, as if her hand bore a sting or were simply unclean.

'Garrett,' she stumbled, not finding the words she had so carefully prepared, 'I left . . . I left because I thought your wife had come back; that Laura was your wife, that there was no place for me; that Bianca was . . .' Her voice broke in a sob, but she kept the tears from her eyes, gazing at him as he loomed over her, his face menacing.

'My wife?' he exclaimed in disbelief.

'Yes,' she said in a soft voice, all energy draining from her. 'I know it's incredible, but I got it wrong. All wrong. Elizabeth told me.' She rose, unable any longer to face this cold mask, and turned towards the door. Just before she opened it, she looked back at him, for what she suddenly felt must be the last time, and saw the drama of expressions playing themselves out on the taut face beneath the shock of white hair. But the eyes fixed on her were still icy.

'I love you, Garrett,' she said simply, 'whatever that may be good for,' and she lurched out, hurrying for the lift, which responded instantly to her touch and carried her away from him, down into what she thought must be the bowels of the earth, the pits of a Danteesque hell.

The icy air outdoors bit into her lungs and as the white flakes clung to everything around her, she felt she was bound for a snowy death as glacial as Garrett's eyes. She walked blindly, wherever the streets led her, her mind frozen into non-existence. After what seemed an eternity she found herself at the SoHo loft, not too sure how she had arrived there. Dimly aware of the frozen hands and feet which seemed to belong to another body, she walked upstairs and without turning on the light, sat huddled, fully dressed on the sofa, her mind as dead as her heart.

She had no idea how much time had passed when she heard a pounding at the door, and prodding stiff limbs into action, she went blankly to open it. Garrett stood there, his face contorted in the half light of the hall by she didn't know what feelings.

'Don't you answer your bell any more?' he raged at her.

She looked at him as if from a great distance, vaguely conscious of the smell of whisky on his breath. He walked past her into the loft, took in the disparity between the lack of lights and her fur coat.

'Have you just come in?' His voice, for reasons she couldn't understand, was bitter.

'It's cold,' she said, shivering, and closed the door behind him, so that the room was again only lit by the unnatural glow of the street lamp.

'Clarissa,' he uttered her name hoarsely, angrily, shaking her by the shoulders so that she was forced to look up at him with dawning memory. Suddenly his lips came down on hers with a painful fury and his arms clasped her fiercely, choking the breath from her. She moaned softly, and abruptly he released her. His face seemed to be sullen, twisted in self-deprecation. Sombrely he questioned her, 'Clarissa, repeat what you said to me this afternoon.'

She moved away from him. 'There's no point.'

'Please, Clarissa!' The words broke from him as if they hurt him.

'Repeat that I'm a fool? That I love you?' she shrugged. 'What's the use? Meaningless facts with no application.' A shudder ran through her, and to still it, she sat down, holding her coat tightly to her.

He watched her closely in the distorted light and then with a stride he was in front of her, his fingers tracing the curve of her cheek, the line of her brow. His face was still grim, his eyes cautious, as they interrogated her.

Then, with a swift movement, he pulled her to him and again his lips sought hers, this time probing her, questioning her, until she trembled against his taut frame. Her arms rose to embrace him and through the heavy wool of his coat she could feel his heart pounding. Her lips opened to him, trying with their pressure to wipe out the pain she had seen in his face, to assuage her own yearning and vanquish unspoken fears.

When their mouths parted, Garrett reached to switch on a lamp. 'I have to look at you, Clarissa.'

She met his eyes forthrightly, responding to his inspection, and as she saw the warmth kindling in his face, an answering pulse seemed to beat in her. She stroked the tense lines in his brow.

'You're pale, little one,' he murmured.

'No paler than you,' she smiled at him wryly. 'It's been a rough time.'

'Very rough,' he acknowledged.

'Shall we take our coats off and have a drink? I think the atmosphere in here is distinctly less chilly.'

A smile flickered across his eyes. 'Ten degrees above zero. I think we can do better than that, don't you, Clarissa?'

'Perhaps.'

'Minx!' He pulled her to him and throwing her coat on the sofa, wrapped his arms round her, pressing her close to him as his hands caressed her. She breathed deeply, taking in the scent of him, the flames beginning to lick at her stomach.

'Twenty degrees,' she laughed, pulling away from him. The brandy should bring it up a little more. She poured a glass for each of them, intensely aware of his eyes on her as she moved round the room. When she sat down opposite him, he looked at her intently.

'Did you really think Laura was my wife?' he said in a low voice.

Clarissa nodded. 'Can you think of any other sane reason for my sudden departure? Though perhaps seeing you with Bianca, after what you'd told me, would have been enough.' She shrugged. 'I assumed that you'd lied to me. That despite what you'd said, you loved her. Why else would you make so many excuses for her? See her, let her touch you?' she shivered. 'After we'd just been . . .' The tears rose in her eyes as she remembered her despair.

'Clarissa,' Garrett chided her, 'Bianca had flown in to plead with me. She was distraught, afraid I'd report her, ruin her career, her life. I said I would do nothing of the kind—though I was sorely tempted. But I did tell her she would have to start looking round for another job. There was no way we could stay in the same firm. I even acknowledged that I might have been partially responsible for the desperation of her action. I was so embroiled with you, I hadn't been treating her very well. And we are old friends, workmates, as I've told you, Clarissa. If you can imagine all that without a few intense glances,' he chuckled, 'a little touching short of murder, then you're not the writer I'd imagined.'

Clarissa looked at him through her tears, wanting to believe him.

'And after you'd seen Bianca with me, you bumped into Laura?' he prodded her.

Clarissa nodded. 'I heard a woman asking for you, announcing herself as Laura Hamilton, I saw Ted rush into her arms,' she grimaced at the recollection. 'So I fled. Marco happened to have come looking for us. How *is* Ted?' She asked after a pause.

Garrett shrugged. 'I think he misses you. Like his father. He knows the cat book off by heart.'

'Did you miss me, Garrett?' Clarissa asked, her voice hardly audible.

'Miss you?' he groaned. 'I've been desolate!' His eyes raked over her. 'I'd show you just how much, but I don't think either of us is in a fit state.'

Suddenly Clarissa felt as if a vast burden had been lifted from her shoulders. She laughed. 'Speak for yourself, Mr Hamilton,' she teased him.

'Come here, you little wildcat. Instantly!' His voice was gruff, but his eyes played with her.

With mock recalcitrance, Clarissa moved to sit by him on the sofa. He looked at her deeply and then kissed her with such passion that she felt the room begin to swerve dizzily round her.

'And now, young lady, it's dreadfully late and I'm going to tuck you into bed so that tomorrow you can talk to me with a degree of sense.' With a deft movement he lifted her into his arms and carried her up the stairs. Clarissa clung to him, unwilling to release him, but he placed her on the bed and then with an infinite gentleness undressed her, kissed her lightly on the breast, and drew the bedclothes up to her neck. His eyes twinkled at her. 'And that, Clarissa Harlowe, is called heroism! I'll see you first thing tomorrow morning, or this morning, I should say.'

Humming to herself, Clarissa put some eggs on to boil and watched the snowflakes dance merrily across her high window. She was ravenous, as if she hadn't eaten for weeks, and the piece of toast she munched greedily tasted like nothing she remembered. The constriction around her chest—which she had thought was the result of the collision—seemed magically to have vanished. She breathed deeply, thinking about nothing in particular, but with the certain knowledge that Garrett would soon be with her. It's enough, she said to herself, blocking out a shadowy doubt which insinuated that presence did not necessarily mean continuity. 'The essence of romance,' she remembered a line from Oscar Wilde, 'is uncertainty.' She chuckled, wondering whether reality might not be preferable.

And then there was Garrett at the door, quite distinctly solid in a capacious leather coat, his handsome face ruddy from the cold.

'Miss me?' his clear eyes questioned her.

Clarissa shook her head. 'I've been far too busy being hungry.' She glanced at him mischievously and flew into his arms.

He held her tightly for a moment, then smacked her bottom. 'Hurry, or the snow will imprison us in New York.'

'Where are we going?'

'Home. To the country.'

'Are you taking the day off?'

'It's Saturday, silly. Don't you writers pay any attention to time?'

Clarissa grinned. 'Only deadlines.'

'Well, you've got five minutes to pack enough gear to last for a week.' Garrett's eyes teased her as she looked at him in astonishment. 'It's Christmas, Clarissa.' He shook his head in disdain. 'That's the trouble with you people who don't have children. No sense of holidays! We'll have to rectify that.'

Her mouth dropped open.

'Four minutes, Clarissa,' he threatened.

She hurried to pull on boots, leg warmers, throw her things into a bag.

'Only a little late,' Garrett smiled at her as she raced down the stairs, and draping an arm casually round her shoulder, he led her down to the car.

'Clarissa!' Two pairs of dark eyes welcomed her from the back of the car.

'In the flesh,' she smiled warmly, and hugged Ted and Elinor. Then, mimicking Garrett's tone, she ordered Elinor into the front seat to attend to the driver, while she huddled into the back with a delighted but slightly shy, Ted.

'Always knew you preferred him.' Garrett murmured with a degree of seriousness which startled her. She made a joke of it.

'I like them young,' she squeezed Ted through the bulk of his enormous snowsuit.

'I'm a robot today,' the little boy announced, as the car moved slowly through the slippery streets.

'What, not a chipmunk?'

'They sleep in winter, silly.'

'Quite right, too,' added Clarissa, watching the thick flakes fall.

'You owe me nine hundred and ninety-nine stories, Clarissa. You remember, don't you?'

Clarissa groaned. 'I'd better start immediately!'

He nodded at her seriously and she began a story which ended only when Ted went off to sleep in her arms.

They drove through the wintry landscape, its contours quite changed in the snow. A hushed stillness seemed to have covered everything, even the slow-moving cars with their white bonnets.

Ted woke just as they pulled up in front of the large house. He looked sleepily up at Clarissa. 'I told you she'd come back, Dad,' he said self-importantly.

'So did I,' Elinor added, turning to face Clarissa. 'And I'm so glad you did.'

'Right, my two prophets,' Garrett said gruffly. 'Off into the house! We have to get an enormous fire going.'

As he lifted the seat back to let Clarissa out of the car, she noticed that his eyes looked dreamy. But he said nothing to her directly.

Clarissa and Elinor busied themselves with preparing a quick hamburger lunch, while Garrett and Ted built an enormous fire in the living room. After lunch, they bundled into innumerable items of clothing—half of which Clarissa borrowed—and trudged off into the woods in search of a tree. It seemed to Clarissa that she could gaze at the untouched snow for hours, but every time she stopped, Garrett urged her on. 'Move, or you'll freeze into position,' he warned, then teased her, 'And I think I distinctly prefer my women alive!'

'Rat!' she murmured.

Indian file, they carried an enormous tree back to the house with them. In a flurry of activity, Garrett brought out a large box of decorations, old and new, all heaped together. Clarissa paused for a moment and watched the little scene.

'You're going to make me sentimental,' she warned Garrett.

He laughed, his face glowing at her. 'As long as you keep it out of your books. It's not a fashionable mode and I'd be forced to cut ruthlessly.'

'Mr Publisher,' she said taunting him.

His eyes flickered over her dangerously and she thought she heard him mutter, 'Later.'

Later turned out to be late indeed, for Ted, in his state of over-excitement, wouldn't settle and it was well after ten before they were alone. Her legs tucked under her, Clarissa sat on the long sofa and gazed into the flames. Garrett placed a coffee laced with brandy in front of her. His eyes seemed sombre.

'Do you resent him, resent Ted, Clarissa? It's not very romantic having a child under one's feet all the time.'

'Resent him?' Clarissa echoed in astonishment, then giggled, remembering his comment in the car. 'Sometimes I think I prefer him!'

The expression on his face as he paced in front of her, his black trousers and thick polo sweater hugging his frame, didn't respond to her tone and she shrugged, looking up at him intently. 'I guess there's been the occasional tinge of resentment—when I've thought you were only putting up with me because Ted seemed to like me, because I was a useful companion for him.'

It was his turn to look astonished. She put a hand out to him and pulled him down beside her. His pupils were black under the thick lashes. She could feel his breath on her face and she trembled.

'I'm a cautious man, Clarissa; layers upon layers of caution.' He looked deeply into her eyes. 'I don't trust women much.'

'That's meant to be my line, the woman's line,' she teased him.

'The sexes, you know, do have some things in common.' A smile flickered over her face at last.

'Suspicion?' she challenged him.

He nodded. 'And this.' His lips searched for her mouth and tenderly, then with a growing, a probing urgency, he kissed her. Clarissa felt the flames stirring deep within her. When he released her, he looked at her for a long moment. Then he cleared his throat, as if what he was about to say disturbed him.

'You're not pregnant, are you, Clarissa?'

Clarissa got up quickly from the sofa. 'Not as far as I know,' she flung at him angrily. 'And if you think that's why I've come back, that I'm anything like that silly, spoiled wife of yours, you can just . . .' at a loss for words, she raged away from him.

'Clarissa,' his hand firmly on her shoulder, he stopped her and caught her in his embrace. His eyes were dark with wanting her. 'I'll try not to spoil you too much,' he murmured.

She wasn't sure she had caught his sense, but when he had led her to his room, he whispered, 'With the woman I love, a child would be no bad thing, Clarissa.'

She felt her pulse set up a wild dancing. 'Me?' she wanted to hear him say it again.

'No,' he shook his head balefully. 'No,' he rained kisses over her face, the soft skin of her throat, and his smile glowed at her. 'The woman I really love is that young English writer—you know, the one who loathes large publishing houses, who always contradicts me, criticises me, flinches when I touch her, tries to murder us all . . . It takes a lot of loving to love all that.'

Gently he unbuttoned her shirt, grazing her skin with his lips, until Clarissa could feel desire surging in her. She trailed her fingers over his chest.

'Yes, it takes a great deal of loving.' He lifted her on to the bed and unzipped her trousers, nuzzling the smooth skin of her stomach with his mouth and then, looking at her with blazing eyes, 'A great deal to convince yourself that you aren't wooing a woman only because your child seems to like her far too much.'

He was lying next to her, his fingers playing over her naked skin, while his eyes trailed over her face.

Clarissa reached for his lips, hungry for their touch. He kissed her lightly, tantalisingly, then stroked the arch of her cheek.

'Yes, and then when you've finally convinced yourself that you're sure, absolutely sure that you love her for all the right reasons,' rakishly he caressed the curve of her hip, 'and she vanishes into the distance with another man, leaving you with only a terse little note which says, "Thanks for the lesson in love," '—Clarissa flinched as he pinched her roughly—'then—then, my little wildcat, you've got to have an enormous reserve of love to convince yourself that she's not just a sensuous little bitch who's used you, used you like another one did.'

'It wasn't like that, Garrett,' Clarissa interrupted him fiercely. 'I was jealous of Bianca, of Laura, of everyone.'

'Just like me.' His eyes sparkled and he slapped her lightly.

'And I thought you were using *me*, for a bet, for a little fling, as a replacement mother, much as I was happy to be one.'

'That's just what I managed to convince myself of yesterday,' he smiled at her. 'But it took one hell of an imaginative leap.'

'A useful faculty for a major publisher,' Clarissa teased him.

'And you, madame writer, you who told me on the very day I met you that writers needed to live alone, do you think you can manage a little company in the house?'

'That depends on who it is and on what it does with its time,' she laughed up at him.

His eyes flared over her and then he kissed her savagely, deeply. 'Will that do?' he whispered huskily.

'Yes,' Clarissa murmured, her heart stirring. A passionate craving coursed through her and she clung to him as if she could never have enough of him, the supple language of his hard, intelligent body, the taut smooth skin which seemed to melt into hers.

'What complicated creatures we are, my love!' she breathed into his flesh, her voice ragged with feeling.

Garrett looked at her, his eyes ablaze in his strong face. 'It will keep us busy with each other for a very long time.'

And as he carried her into a region beyond words, Clarissa knew that at last she had perhaps learned something of love.

Coming next month in Harlequin Romance!

2647 TIME TO FORGET Kerry Allyne
Their families have been feuding for generations. So why does a
young Australian woman join forces with a man from the other
side?

2648 A DAMAGED TRUST Amanda Carpenter
Colorado's rugged beauty and a very determined man challenge a
disillusioned young woman to face her fears and trust once more in
her ability to distinguish love from illusion.

2649 MOON LADY Jane Donnelly
When a man who usually gets what he wants has his eye on a piece
of land owned by a woman who doesn't like him, what will he do?
Why, he'll turn on the charm, of course.

2650 RIVIERA ROMANCE Marjorie Lewty
A legal secretary doesn't wish to tangle with a ruthless lawyer she
meets in the romantic Riviera. Especially not when he's sure to find
her guilty... guilty of love.

2651 A WOMAN IN LOVE Lilian Peake
Is it merely guilty conscience that prompts a man to offer his
secretary another job after firing her from his London ad agency?
No! Not when he wants to employ her... as his wife!

2652 SOUL TIES Karen Van Der Zee
An American woman working in Indonesia recognizes a man she's
met—and loved! She can't understand why he denies knowing her.
And she can't accept his engagement to another woman.

BARBARA DELINSKY
Fingerprints

Carly Quinn is a
woman with a past.
Born Robyn Hart, she
was forced to don a new
identity when her intensive
investigation of an arson-ring
resulted in a photographer's death
and threats against her life.

Ryan Cornell's entrance into her life
was a gradual one. The handsome
lawyer's interest was piqued, and then
captivated, by the mysterious Carly—a
woman of soaring passions and a
secret past.

RIDE A PAINTED PONY

by BEVERLY SOMMERS
The third
HARLEQUIN AMERICAN ROMANCE
PREMIER EDITION

A prestigious New York City publishing company decides to launch a new historical romance line, led by a woman who must first define what love means.